Water Flowing Over Stone

Water flowing over Stone

stories and inventions by Cerek

Yggdrasil Books
1999

First Edition, March 1999
10   9   8   7   6   5   4   3   2   1

ISBN 0-9667513-9-6 Trade Paperback
ISBN 0-9667513-8-8 Limited deluxe
Library of Congress Catalog Card Number 98-75007
Printed in the United States of America

For information, contact
Yggdrasil Books
Box 399
Waldron, Washington USA-98297

Contents

Water, Stone: Dreams, Bones

The Greatest Show

Water, Stone: Dreams, Bones

Gigi

Gigi the Singer came to us this morning exhausted, all wet and covered with mud. She had been out all night, flying about the mountain crags singing. It had been howling and blowing rain for five days straight; few of us had even ventured outside the caves, to hunt the Smallfolk that we depend on for our sustenance. Instead we lay huddled beside the huge bodies of our Old Ones, who keep us warm during the Cold Season, and even feed us from their own flesh when all else fails.

Gigi will certainly die before the evening falls. Already she lays struggling for breath on the stony floor, shivering from time to time with exhaustion, and from other agonies too, no doubt. The Feeders come by on their rounds, try to tempt her with tasty though meager morsels, but she declines. She really seems to have no interest, seems content to end her life today.

She has always been a foolish one. The Seasons of the World, the murmurs of the Mountains and the Winds, she seems not to hear. Or she certainly hears them, but she hears other things besides, things from inside of herself no doubt, which must be stronger than what we hear, and it is this calling that she heeds. So last night — evening had just fallen — Gigi rouses herself, shakes out her wings, and makes as if to go out. "What do, Gigi?" one or two ask, glad probably to have a diversion from the monotony of our evenings. "Out to fly, out to sing." The response seems disinterested, as if we really are not here, as if speaking to herself perhaps.

Out? ... Fly? ... Sing? ... Hardly anyone has been out for five days. A tempest rages. Gales rip into our mountains. We can hear the winds clearly from our caves and it disturbs our rest. Only a few Hunters have ventured out, without eagerness, driven by the Tribe's hunger. And these have flown as little as possible, contenting themselves with climbing up cliff-faces, searching out the dwelling-holes of the Smallfolk, then ferreting them out with long tongues and much trickery. One does not fly in such weather. But to sing? We do not sing, only Gigi sings. We hear her sometimes, this strange rustling, grating, rumbling sound that she calls 'singing'. We don't laugh — we know it's Gigi, no need to laugh. Some have tried to mimic her out of curiosity. She doesn't care. She doesn't care if we laugh or if we try to mimic her. She hardly hears those of the Tribe, just as she hardly hears the Seasons, the Storms, the Earth's Rumbling.

So in the midst of the terrible tempest, Gigi goes out one evening to sing. No one would try to stop her, of course. With anyone else one might try to argue, but with Gigi all know it is useless, she hears other voices.

Does anyone even hear her singing? Not the Storm, it howls relentlessly, drowning out all other sound. Certainly not the Smallfolk, they cower in their tiny holes like we in our caves, awaiting a break in the weather, awaiting the return of the Calm. The rocks? Can rocks hear? The Earth's Rumbling moves them, but can they hear our voices? Maybe it is the rocks that hear Gigi. But most likely, no one and nothing hears Gigi sing. We doubt even that she hears herself sing. Something inside her hears, no doubt, but her own voice is likely as uninteresting to her as much of the rest of the World.

So she has spent the night outside, singing amidst the Storm. Death certainly lies near for her. She stumbled in this morning as the Light was just forming. We said nothing, watched her stumble across the cave to her own corner, gasping, clearly exhausted, worse than exhausted. Two tribesones went to warm her, cradled her body in theirs for hours, crooned our tribal croon. Gigi said nothing, acknowledged nothing. Yes, you had to sing, I think to myself, opposite her in the half-darkness. It will kill you, but you had to sing. I thought for a long time about the nature of this singing, tried even to hear her song a little in my mind, but still I understood nothing. If I understood, would I then want to sacrifice myself for the singing also, forget all else, abandon all to this folly? But then it would not be folly if I understood it ... No, I did not wish to understand! Let Gigi kill herself! Let us all forget that we ever heard of this singing. It brings us nothing. It would be the end of the Tribe if we were all to begin singing.

I thought for many long hours. I still lay thinking when Gigi died. One last hoarse gasp, then silence. It was dark again, and I could not even make out her shape. We would take her out in the morning, drag her to the burying crevasse. I felt a sudden pang of disappointment; I realized that I had been hoping to hear her sing one last time, just one final time. In my mind I tried to reconstruct the strange sound of her song. Maybe, maybe I could manage to sing a small part of it myself ...

Stone-Woman, Silver-Man

"Elzira ... Elzira ..." The voice drifted in through the open back door, a low, humming drone coming from the barley fields that lay twenty paces beyond the house. They were calling her again from out there. But Elzira's mother was still waiting for her inside. Elzira quickly found and brought back the implements that had been requested from the back room. Her mother and two sisters were busily engaged in soapmaking at the stove and the big plank table where the family ate. Another sister and her brother worked in the next room with their father, who sat bent over his shoemaking last. The two central rooms of the house were filled with lamplight and the low, steady murmur of voices. Everyone else in the family was occupied by their evening work. Elzira, at seven the youngest, was called upon from time to time to fetch things for them. She quietly handed her mother the tools and slipped out again.

She sat down on the back stoop, looking out into the deepening darkness, as if expecting them to call her name again. But she had heard it the first time, she knew they were there. From behind her, one lone oil lamp in the back room cast a weak yellow light, barely revealing the path that led back to the fields.

"I'm coming," she said in her mind. She knew she didn't have to say it aloud.

After a few moments her eyes had adjusted better to the darkness. She got up and walked down the path, into the rows of grain that now stood above her head. She felt — older? That was the only label she had been able to put onto the strange, unworldly feeling she got when she went out to visit the corn-people. She had always been the baby of the family: her nearest sister was twelve. At home, she was of little account, mutely helped when asked, but was given no real responsibilities. But out here, in the fields, she felt different — older, perhaps.

She felt the little hands take hers, one on each side. They seemed the hands of a tiny child; they seemed the hands of some unknown animal.

But they were just the corn-people.

They treated her with deference; she had no fear of them at all. They had been calling to her, and she had been visiting them for nearly a year. It had been happening more and more as summer progressed. Late in the spring, on some whim, she had brought out with her one of the small wheels of hard, sheep cheese that lay curing on the top shelf of the back room. When she presented it, she heard the sound of many voices murmuring together amongst the rows — approval, it seemed. The next night when she came, she was offered a little platter of moist, sweet, barley cakes. The cakes were good, though ordinary. The platter was made of finely wrought metal filagree; Elzira wanted to examine it closely, but it was whisked away before she had a chance.

It was shortly after that night that she started finding things. It began with household objects that her family had mislaid — her sister's ring, one of her father's knives. She didn't look for them. Her mother might say, "Has anyone seen my thimble?" and then Elzira, a few minutes later, might discover it beneath the chair that she had been using. It took only a few times for her family to take notice. At first they joked about it, but then they kept their silence. Now they often asked her to fetch things for them, no longer being sure to mention where the object might be. Had they also noticed that Elzira was wandering around in the barley fields long after dark? They did not ask her about it.

Later, she started finding other things, outside the house, around the yard and garden. First, a silver chain, which she gave to her mother, who exclaimed over it profusely. Then a strange coin, which her father carefully cleaned and polished with spittle and boot-oil and leather, then stared at, puzzled, for a long time; at length he declared that it was not the coin of any land that he had ever heard of. Elzira did not know what finally became of it.

When she found the stone carving, she kept it to herself. She knew it would only unsettle her family. It was a woman's face carved into a rock which she had unearthed while digging in the garden. It seemed very old, but the fine lines were still distinct.

She kept the rock wrapped up in a square of cloth behind a cross-piece in the wooden wall next to her bed. From time to time she studied it in private. The woman's hair was wavy and her eyes had a different, not-quite-right shape to them. The lips were pursed as if saying something. Elzira kept wanting to know what it was. And looking at it also gave her that strange feeling. Not until much later did it occur to her that the rock had something to do with the corn-people.

The summer rains were late. It had been dry since late winter and the fields were parched and stunted. At midsummer, her grandmother presented her, as the youngest granddaughter, with an elaborately worked leather box. Inside were special sweets in the shape of large barley-corns. Elzira offered each member of her family one of the corns as was expected of her. But then, rather than keep the rest for herself, she left the box and its contents out in the rows. It was gone the next day. In its place was a tiny bag of some sheer material like silk, stuffed with real barley corns, and some of the largest that Elzira had ever seen. Later (she didn't know why) she walked up the little hillock that dominated their fields and scattered the fat grains there.

Some days later, Elzira stood beside her father as he tended the rows of stunted plants. "I wonder if it will rain soon," she remarked to no one in particular. Her father looked forlornly up at the clear, coppery sky and made no reply.

But the following day dawned unexpectedly cool and grey, and before morning was spent, the clouds opened up. The summer rains had arrived, late but abundantly. Two months later, the stalks were tall and juicy, the heads fat with ripening grain. The summer's growth more than made up for the spring's drought.

Now, on a late-summer night, Elzira followed the corn-people once more into the rows. It had been a hot, sultry day. The night air was sweet with the scent of the ripening seeds, mingled with the musk of the rich, moist earth. Elzira followed where she was led; the little hands of the corn-people were soft but firm. She never wondered that she did not see them at all. Soon it seemed like they were going down, down ... She looked up, thinking to see sky, ragged clouds broken with stars, but there was only blackness above her. The little hands tugged more insistently at hers ...

Afterwards she found herself lying on the ground. She lay still for a long time, breathing calmly and blinking her eyes, as if blinking away heavy sleep. Now there *were* clouds breaking across the sky; some bit of moonlight lit them weakly from above. She knitted her brow in concentration, trying to piece together the dream images that lingered ... A room filled with strange people, friendly and hospitable, all talking to each other and to her. But she could not recall any of their words. The faces, when she tried to focus on them, seemed just beyond her recall. She had seen some of them before, she was sure.

She rose, and only then noticed the object that she held in her closed hand. She walked out from the rows so she could see it better. It glistened silvery in the faint moonlight. It was smooth and metallic and warm from her touch. It was a little cast figure, a man (she thought) with a prominent nose and eyes and an odd hat. His lips were curled up into an uncertain smile. The eyes were shaped like the eyes of the stone woman. His arms, crossed in front of him, bore full sheaths of barley, which covered up his body and whose heads framed his face. The feeling, looking at it, was the same that she felt with stone-woman, but now she began to poke at the edges of that feeling, though she lacked the words to help her. Stone-woman, silver-man, the corn-people, the meeting last night under the ground — all of these were part of this feeling. She felt herself, without warning, as tiny as a tiny grain of barley resting on an enormous hillside with the winds sweeping over and around her. Then she felt herself floating in blackness; the stars above her were far away and icy, but made tiny, crackling sounds as they shone. And she no longer knew if she was as tiny as a grain or as huge as the limitless earth. Her throat contracted for a moment with fear, then a deep calm settled over her and — once more she was standing at the edge of the fields, holding the little silver man in her hand.

She went inside. Her mother was just putting away her pots and tools. Her sisters and brother had gone to bed. Her father's work-lamp was also out. No one asked her where she had been. She laid silver-man beside stone-woman and went to sleep. She slept soundly and without further dreams.

A few days later, her father declared the fields ripe for

reaping, and all that morning the house was filled with the clang of metal and the sharpening of scythes. Her father and sisters and brother came in briefly at midafternoon and Elzira and her mother presented them with refreshment. The dirt floors of the house were starting to be littered again with the dried barley stalks and heads, as they would be for weeks.

Elzira set about stoking the cooking fire while her mother mixed and kneaded the loaves for tonight's dinner. But Elzira's thoughts were elsewhere — something was troubling her, but what? and she became careless with the stove. Suddenly, she cried out in pain: she had just seared an ugly mark across the inside of her left forearm. It was a long, thin, red mark such as a scythe might make.

Her mother, who had been watching, scolded her. Elzira said nothing; she knew she had been careless. She held her arm in a bucket of cool washwater until the pain subsided, then went into the bedroom where she found a jar of salve among her sisters' baskets. After she had smeared some onto her arm, she suddenly thought of her hidden treasures and took them out from the wall for a moment. She stared at stone-woman's lips; she could almost, almost make out the word there. Silver-man's mouth no longer looked to her like it was smiling. The eyes of both figures seemed to be beseeching her. Suddenly she thrust both of them back into their nook, and ran out of the room, past her mother, and out of the house.

The fields nearest the house had all been cleared and already lay gathered up into loose sheaves. Off to her left, the two oldest sisters were advancing toward the willow grove and to the right, a sister and the brother were nearing the brook. Straight ahead of her, her father worked alone, working his way up towards the little hillock that dominated their fields. The sun beat down steadily today out of an almost cloudless sky. There was a low humming sound in the air ...

Elzira was running towards her father. Her sisters said she shouted, but she remembered nothing. She seized her father's arms and stopped his swinging. He was merely puzzled and surprised at first, not angry. Elzira wanted him to stop cutting; she did not seem to mind if he cut on this side or that side, but she insisted that he stop cutting upon the hillock. She was very clear and firm about this. He laughed at first, questioned her a bit, but when he saw how serious she was, he laid down his scythe and called the other children over to him.

All of them had stopped by now, too, and were staring at the strange scene. Elzira's father paced out a boundary (with Elzira's coaching) and told them in a very final way that they were not to cut beyond it. His tone of voice was such that no one asked him why. They all went back to their work and by dinnertime had finished all the fields on that side of the brook.

That evening around the table everyone seemed especially spent, and the conversation was muted. Elzira, often a very quiet child anyway, was lost in her thoughts and said nothing.

All their grain was cut and stored away before the rains came again. The harvest had been bountiful and nothing had spoiled. No one spoke of the grain that had been left standing on the hillock.

Elzira kept the two figures to herself for many years, before finally giving them to her great-granddaughter who was also known as a wanderer among the rows. Though they are worn by the centuries, Elzira's descendants still keep them to this day, and sometimes still try to read the words on the lips of stone-woman, or to interpret the curious smile — if that is what it is — on silver-man's face. The grain on the hillock has never been cut again.

In the Hall of the Weavers

"Qass ... Qass ... QASS!"

Not until the third time did Kirleen get his friend's attention. With the slightest reluctance Qass removed his viewing lenses in response to Kirleen's salutation. It seemed to take him a moment to refocus his eyes on the colleague in front of him. Those eyes! Kirleen has always been struck by the younger man's face. It seemed such a babyish face, with its smooth, high, untroubled brow; it was fringed by a curly, sandy mane of fine hair. But Qass's deepset eyes seemed somehow ancient. They were such a clear, deep, transparent green, and they looked like they were filled with the sea — the ancient, restless, yet unchanging sea.

It was a full holiday but Qass sat here anyway in the Guild Hall of the Weavers and Makers. For months now, he had been spending most of his spare time engrossed in his personal endeavor, the dream-crystal weaving machine. That is what the other Guild members called it; Qass himself had some more arcane term.

"What are you doing here?" asked Qass, a little dreamily. He had evidently been playing with his machine for a while this morning. It always gave him a certain dreamy, faraway air.

"I might ask you the same," responded Kirleen, "but of course I can see. I only came to pick up my bag. How is the work going today?"

The younger man was always eager to talk about his work. Kirleen could readily understand less than half of it. He was primarily a Weaver. He could use the machines skillfully and even repair them serviceably, but mechanical innovation was not his strength. Qass on the other hand was a Master Artificer — both a Master Weaver *and* a Master Builder — but as a Builder he was unsurpassed. Given what he had already accomplished at 33, people commented that he would surely be known as one of the greatest Builders ever.

Qass brightened at the question, smiled sweetly, like a small child. Tiny wrinkles appeared at the corners of his ancient eyes, in the otherwise smooth face.

"Take a look for yourself, Kirleen," he said, and proffered him the viewing cap with the lenses.

Kirleen put them on. As accustomed as he was to the weaving machines, there was always the little adjustment as the solid world slipped away and a different reality came into view. But this was not an ordinary weaving machine. There was not the usual geometric regularity of a myriad of strands of different colors and sizes and shapes; it was instead a shimmering chaos. At Qass's prompting he let his eyes relax. Soon the chaos resolved itself into something like a swarm of shifting crystals. It was confusing and difficult to focus on; it made his head swim.

After a few minutes Kirleen took the lenses off and handed them to Qass. "It's very lovely," he said, admiringly, "but too hard for me to follow. And none of it's real?"

"Real?" repeated Qass, with a bemused, tinkling laugh. "Real?" He said no more, but clearly, his mind examined and toyed with the thought ...

Kirleen knew that it was not real in the same way that what he saw through the magnifying lenses of an ordinary weaving machine was real. Kirleen worked with these everyday; he was a master craftsman and used them to produce works of art prized around the world. Three hundred years ago, the Guild produced unequaled woven tapestries on hand-powered looms. Then, over the span of one generation, the first machines were built and with them the Craft changed forever. Although there were still a handful of artisans who produced tapestries in the traditional fashion, laying the strands on by hand, one by one, the Guild now produced a far richer and more subtle array of products. With the powerful lenses, infinitesimal manipulating needles, use of exotic materials, today's Weavers made objects that bore little resemblance at all to the old tapestries. And so the title "Makers" was added to the name of their profession. Some of their works looked like they had been carved from iridescent stone, others were soft and yielding, comforting and warm. Still others mimicked natural objects or artifacts. Many were functional as well as beautiful, others purely ornamental, some totally abstract. All were as highly prized as the tapestries of old.

Perhaps in some way, Qass's new machine was the ultimate development of the Weaver's art. It produced no real product at all. There were no holding stands, no magnifying lenses, no manipulating needles. What one saw through the lenses was just a trick of light, an illusion. Yet this illusion could be recreated precisely, if with difficulty, and now — according to Qass — it was possible to record on magnetic tablets the thousands of tiny steps and adjustments required to recreate such a pattern. The tablets were real and solid, so in a way, perhaps, the illusion was just as real and solid.

They had had these discussions before, many times. Qass had expounded on his novel views at length. Today he just said, in his laughing, tinkling tones, "real?" and let it rest at that.

"Your images certainly look different today," said Kirleen, continuing the conversation. "They seem more complex somehow, yet also not as clear as before, more chaotic perhaps ..."

"Complex? Chaotic? Yes, they are all of that. I've been filling in more detail. I have discovered a number of tricks to simplify my work, ways to repeat patterns and the like. I am also playing around with randomness ..."

He became distracted by some thought, by some new idea perhaps, and stared silently into space for many seconds. Kirleen, absorbed in his own plans for the day, finally ended their conversation. "Well, I must meet Illien at the upper stairs. I hope you will show me more of your new work when it's further along."

Qass blinked and stared at him in confusion, as if surprised to see him there. "Yes, certainly," he said, although he could not clearly recall what they had been talking about. "Yes, certainly — certainly I will."

* * * * *

A week, two weeks went by. Kirleen did not see Qass much, or only in passing, although he was aware of him on occasion, heard his name mentioned not infrequently. He knew that Qass was more and more engrossed in his private endeavor. He was still called upon on occasion when a machine needed an unusual or particularly subtle adjustment or repair, and so far as Kirleen knew, he responded to such requests promptly and effectively. But Kirleen also realized that his friend was being called upon less and less frequently. There was a general understanding amongst the Weavers that Qass was involved in something very important, albeit arcane and incomprehensible, and ought not to be disturbed. Even the Master of the Guild Hall, an indomitable woman named Esmant, whose suggestions had nearly the force of law, even she let Qass be. The aura of genius that had sometimes touched him, now became almost palpable, and he was clearly answerable to no one. In the past, Esmant had complained wryly of the uselessness of Qass's invention; now she kept her silence, watched and waited like everyone else.

Late one afternoon, Kirleen came through the Old Room where Qass labored in a corner workshop. This room was the most ancient of all the rooms of the Guild Hall. It had last been rebuilt twelve hundred years ago; no one knew when it had first been built or by whom. The wooden floor was worn smooth and shiny by the footfall of generations of Weavers. It was near the end of the day; late afternoon sunlight streamed in through the tall, multipaned window crystals. Kirleen had just delivered a boxful of notes and sketches to the archivist for recording and safekeeping, completing a particularly demanding project that had involved a dozen Weavers. He was tired but content, unhurried, at his leisure. He spotted Qass near the forming lathe that he used to fabricate parts for his dream-crystal weaving machine. The handful of workers still in the spacious, high-ceilinged workroom were just leaving. Qass sat alone in a little sitting alcove under the open windows. He sat by himself, quiet and likewise unhurried; lost in thought, but with an air of taking his ease.

Kirleen approached his friend cordially. They had both been exceedingly busy of late and had not spoken for more than a week. "Greet thee, brother Builder," began Kirleen, using one of the customary salutations. Qass looked up, startled out of his reverie, then smiled his gentle, endearing smile.

"Greet thee, Weaver and friend Kirleen." Kirleen sat himself down on the settee beside his friend, who immediately proffered him tea from the ever present flagon. The two men sipped for a few moments in silence.

"It's been a busy week for me," began Kirleen. "You also?" Qass smiled and nodded. He looked tired, but satisfied. "You've been working on the dream machine, I venture?"

"Most of the week ..." He seemed inclined to be sociable, but spoke hesitantly at first, as one unused to speech. Gradually his words gathered momentum. "... that last attempt was all nonsense — just a blind alley — but this time, this time ..." The faraway look came back to his eyes, the strange satisfied smile curled his lips. "Yes, I think I am really onto something this time, Kirleen; I know it! You see, I am really quite a cautious person, but I am completely convinced of my direction now — it feels right. It is so elegant, so obvious now that I see it ..."

"And all your earlier work?"

Qass laughed his tinkling laugh. "Foolish stuff," he said bemused, taking another sip of the cup he held. "Very solid, very carefully constructed work, but too controlled, too ... deterministic!" Kirleen just listened attentively. "I calculated the other week — with optimistic assumptions and using all of the shortcuts that I have worked out — I calculated that in order to even approximate the degree of detail that we can detect — just with our unaided senses — in this world we live in — to construct just one small piece of such a world would take — using my previous methods — you want to guess? — No, I won't even ask you to guess! — it would take approximately five billion years! Five billion!" He laughed again; he truly found it amusing.

"So I concluded that I was at a dead end, that I would just be able to create beautiful crystalline patterns — works of art, no doubt, interesting no doubt — but hardly a complete world ..."

"A world? What do you mean, world?"

"Yes, yes! You see, it's obviously impossible, don't you, using such crude techniques?"

Kirleen saw nothing of the sort, but let his friend continue.

"So something entirely different was needed, a whole new approach, something ... radical! And then, suddenly, it was all so obvious." He paused, not for effect, but to contemplate or to savor this obvious, elegant solution that he now saw so clearly before him.

"It's not obvious to me, Qass." Kirleen's mind seemed to be drifting off, trying somehow to follow Qass's unspoken thoughts.

"Oh, but it will be, it will be! ... You see, I felt stymied also. The problem seemed so intractable, my ambition — overweening. How possibly to construct an entire world — a world! — as complex as this one, in anything less than the time that ours took to come about. Impossible?"

"You are surely speaking of illusions again, certainly not a real world, certainly not as we Weavers make things ..."

"Real? Illusion? Really, Kirleen, I no longer know the difference. Do you? Do you really?" He spoke with a strange conviction.

Kirleen was silent, troubled in his mind, confused by the direction their conversation was taking. He was exhausted and felt strangely unreal himself, as if floating in space. He found it difficult to pay attention to his friend's explanations. Qass's face and his voice seemed immensely far away.

"... not five billion years, but five weeks or months ... was it merely a question of scale? ... creating a unique local physics, at an infinitesimal level ... of course, it means giving up absolute control, but that was a dead end ... to set up the basic laws, then let it evolve ... watch what's happening, intervene from outside, perhaps even change the laws from time to time ... slightly, of course ... how difficult to find a stable system? ..."

From far away, mixed with Qass's laughter, came the chime of silvery bells, three groups of three, then a final chime. Kirleen started out of a dream, a dream of walking an endless beach of pure white sand, beside a strangely quiet sea. The bells were summoning them to the evening meal in the commons. Qass's voice still rambled on softly nearby, like a magical incantation, in that ancient room, beneath the high windows.

"... requiring a lot of attention at the beginning, if it's going to evolve into anything interesting. I've really not slept at all these last five nights. But I seem to have plenty of energy ..."

"So this 'world' of yours, you have actually made a start?" asked Kirleen, trying to pick up the thread of their conversation.

"Yes — yes, indeed! Would you like to take a look?"

"Surely — well ... briefly. The evening bell has just rung. Will you join me at commons?"

"Not tonight. Come, put the lenses on for a moment!"

Kirleen followed Qass to his machine, put the cap with the heavy lenses over his head, his fingers automatically seeking the control levers. Qass put on a similar cap. All Kirleen saw was darkness. Perhaps here and there were faint points of light — or perhaps it was his own eyes deceiving him.

"We will need to go down at least eleven levels to see anything interesting," said Qass's voice, now disembodied.

"Eleven?" questioned Kirleen. The ordinary machines could only achieve five or six levels, ample for the most intricate weaving.

"Correct. It is only possible for my plan to work on an infinitesimal scale. This machine has 33 levels ..."

Kirleen pushed the levers. Now the darkness was punctuated by fuzzy yet unmistakable balls of light. Qass guided his hand on the levers; together they navigated through the darkness; some of the lights passed behind them and others came into view. There were slight differences in their sizes and colors.

"... billions of these tiny points. I have given up trying to count them. I could not conceivably control them all; that's the very basis of my design, you see — so I focus on a few, change conditions slightly, observe ... Like this one."

The lever clicked several levels more — 13, 14, 15 ... Part of Kirleen's mind tried to compute the magnitude, then gave up, reeling. There was certainly no doubt that Qass was a genius.

One of the fuzzy points of light became a distinct disc; smaller and faintly luminous balls seemed to be swarming nearby.

"We can go down farther," said Qass's voice as three more bells sounded, at an immense distance. He brought one of the smaller balls to the center, pressed the lever further. Kirleen felt himself suddenly sinking, falling ...

Kirleen pulled the lenses from his eyes abruptly, ending his fall. "Enough," he said in a somewhat shaken voice, "enough for now. I will observe more later, Qass."

Qass removed his own slowly, almost reluctantly. "It is beautiful, is it not?" he asked, smiling radiantly.

"Beautiful!"

* * * * *

That was the last conversation Kirleen had with the Master Artificer Qass. During the following week Kirleen passed through that part of the hall several times, on purpose, just to check on his friend. He was frankly worried. Early or late, Qass sat by his machine, working, his lenses on.

Kirleen thought to speak to him, but each time the intensity of the man's concentration was so great that he could not bring himself to do so. He realized with some alarm that he had not seen Qass at commons for several weeks. He noticed that the other three work places in the Old Room were now idle; no one chose to work alongside the genius builder, now so consumed by his genius.

When Kirleen heard the voice of Esmant, the Master of the Hall, screaming one morning as he entered, he knew in his heart what had happened.

"Qass dead! Qass dead! The machine has killed him!" she wailed. Kirleen's stomach knotted, his heart pounded, even as he heard the inevitable news.

A small circle of onlookers stood around Qass's corner when Kirleen arrived, staring. Kirleen was the first one to approach the slumped-over figure and remove the lenses. As he did so, he locked the controls so that they would not be changed. His friend's eyes were already closed; he carried the emaciated body to the settee and arranged the limbs in a seemly fashion, as if Qass were resting. It seemed as if the poor fellow must not have eaten for weeks ...

Esmant, grieving and raging, wanted to destroy the machine immediately. She, Master of the Hall, doubtless felt responsible for the dead man. Kirleen, shaken but determined, prevented her. It should be kept as a monument, he argued, kept but never used again. That corner should be left as it was as a perpetual memorial to the Guild's greatest Builder.

In the end, he prevailed. The machine was left alone; a simple, rough-hewn border of stone was placed around Qass's workplace to set it apart. The deeds of the dead man were recounted and recorded by the archivist. Qass's frail body was burned and the ashes scattered to nourish the wildflowers beside the pool in the Guild's innermost garden.

Weeks passed. The work of the Guild of Weavers and Makers went on. Eventually Weavers even began using the weaving machines near Qass's memorial again. Late one day — long after everyone else had left the hall — Kirleen stepped into the Old Room. The twilight sifted in through the still open windows. Unhesitatingly, he stepped over the low stone border, sat down at Qass's work bench and pulled the lenses over his eyes. The controls, he saw, were still locked into the position where Qass had left them. Kirleen's eyes adjusted to the new scene. A small, colored ball floated in the darkness near the center of the viewing area. Kirleen pushed the lever further and fell, fell ...

Soon he was looking down upon a beach, a beach of white, white sand. The sea beside it was oddly calm, but not completely so: a weak tide pulled its surface into gentle waves. The water was darkish, murky, and his eyes could not penetrate very far into it. But, already, he could see fleet, shadowy things stirring in its depths. The quietness was deceiving: a quietness before a beginning ...

Kirleen pulled off the viewing cap, snapped off its fittings, and strode out of the room, into the gathering dusk.

The Gift of Al Shagat

Carpenter's ship exploded, somewhere deep in space. The cause of the explosion was never established, but a number of seemingly random, unrelated facts proved to be crucial to the aftermath: One, Carpenter had been prospecting in the Reeses and was transporting a load of xenoperli back to the Periphery. Two, his cat Hominy was travelling with him. And lastly, a Creator happened to be passing through that region of space at the time of the explosion.

Xenoperli, also known as mind manna, also known as fool's wisdom, also known by a score of other names, are the almost legendary excreta of certain, primitive colonial organisms of Esmarillis Quatorce. They are complex, organic, crystalline structures in the form of tiny, darkly iridescent beads which are extruded by bryzoan colonies in response to irritation by foreign particles, environmental stress, etc. They are roughly analogous to the pearls produced by terrestrial mollusks. When worn on the human body as jewelry, they will induce unusual psychic experiences, even in those not ordinarily susceptible to such phenomena. In close proximity to someone already possessing active or latent psychic abilities, the effect of xenoperli can be devastating; and in the hands of anyone but the most skilled psi practitioner, may lead to madness in the wearer, and physical and emotional damage to anyone nearby. Their importation has now been banned by the Directorate, and the possession of already existing xenoperli is strictly controlled.

Enrique Carpenter's cat Hominy reportedly always travelled with him. This was not only in violation of numerous Guard regulations, but contrary to any kind of common sense. It was inappropriate, unwise, and downright dangerous. It was doubly dangerous to have such a creature along while travelling through the dimensionally poorly charted spaces around the Reeses. And apparently the creature was not confined, anesthetized, or de-reified in any fashion. It may even have been sitting on his lap.

So the ship exploded. The cause at this point is irrelevant. The only important details were the cat and the xenoperli. And doubtless, the whole event would have passed practically unnoticed to anyone except for the presence of a Creator.

We do not know what Creators are. But we do know that they can manipulate matter in ways that still defy our understanding of physics. We believe that they are not very numerous, that they are terribly ancient, and that they are possibly sentient. This last statement is the most controversial. To our instruments they look like little more than concentrations of extremely dense matter, with a characteristic radiative signature. It has proven almost impossible to study them in any systematic fashion. They behave as if they possess a very detailed map of universal space, down to more dimensions than we can accurately measure. They come and they go — disappear and reappear — in unpredictable patterns. Scientists have long attempted to follow them, but that is only possible as long as they stay in three dimensions, which rarely happens for more than hours at a time. Once they disappear from three-space, it's impossible to tell where they will turn up again.

So what we know of the Creators is largely the accumulation of accidental, unplanned observations. Like any superconcentrated mass, it can also be dangerous to come too close to them, but in their case it is also dangerous to attract their attention by unusual (that is to say, sentient) behavior. The results of that can only be called unpredictable. It is due to the strange, sometimes radical, changes that they can make in nearby objects during a multi-dimensional transition that their name derives.

Our name for them is certainly highly suggestive. Many indeed ascribe divine powers to them, and believe that they involve themselves intimately in human affairs. However, our best minds, to this day, cannot even agree if they are sentient or a mere physical phenomenon. Or whether these are even mutually exclusive possibilities.

A shipment of psi-genic crystals, a cat, a Creator. Three seemingly unrelated facts. They may in fact be unrelated, but a Special Investigator's Report to the Directorate suggests otherwise. The Coefficient of Strangeness (asserts the report) would otherwise be utterly astronomical. So we are forced to the conclusion that the Creator did it, that it somehow manipulated the products of the explosion in a very unusual fashion. However, the consequences of this presumed intervention were not discovered for another thirty-five years, and not widely known for fifty. Today, the result is an accepted part of our culture, albeit a very bizarre one ...

On the fourth and outermost planet of the rather isolated sun Rigas Cazoli (the name means nothing; it is merely a computer generated mnemonic label) there lives a hundred-meter high psychic cat. Both the words "cat" and "lives" are certainly misnomers, but they probably approximate reality as well as any other terms. This cat-like creature, externally, is remarkably like a classic Terran *felis catus domesticus*, only vastly larger. The long, fluffy, pale-pink fur is an iridescent blue near the tips, a combination that has never been obtained in recorded cat-breeding. However, other than the unusual color and gigantic size, the overall physical description, as far as we can tell, is almost identical to that of Enrique Carpenter's cat Hominy, even down to the rare, six-toed forepaws.

The differences, of course, are legion. The giant psi-cat, whom pilgrims call Al Shagat (the origins of this name are unclear) breathes a mixture of methane and phosphene and lives in an environment of 60 to 100 degrees below zero Celsius. These conditions seem to be its only physical requirements. It appears neither to take food into itself nor to excrete any waste product other than vapors. Not surprisingly, it is the only inhabitant of this planet.

For most of the seven-year orbital cycle of its planet, Al Shagat remains in a reposing position, but for a substantial number of months each cycle, it runs wildly about the planet's surface, leaping and kicking and digging feverishly. Pilgrims stay away during these periods; the cat, if approached, can be deadly. But the rest of the time it sits, quietly and innocuously, like an enormous sphinx, and receives visitors from across the stars.

They come by the thousands each month, in spite of the rigors, of the expense of the journey, of the dangers inherent in landing and surviving on such an uninviting planetary surface. The atmosphere is poisonous; temperature and pressure are extreme. Complex and expensive equipment is required for survival. But still they come. On any given day, several hundreds may be in attendance. It is like a religious gathering, or an oracle, even an imperial audience. People come with their problems, with their questions, even with their infirmities. Sometimes they don't even know why they have come.

Few — perhaps none — ever leave unsatisfied.

Many experience some kind of turning point in their

lives. Contrary to some claims, it can hardly be called a religious experience. However, it is certainly intense, deeply personal, and ineffable. Questions are answered; doubts and confusion are dissolved away; lives find direction. It is true: some few do not return; their minds or bodies are not equal to the experience. Madness or death are genuine hazards of an encounter with Al Shagat.

What actually happens at these oracles? The Special Investigator's Report did not even attempt to say. The most definite answers come from those who have not experienced it personally. The Guard long ago issued a traveller's advisory warning of disorientation, psychic distress, and possible physical or mental damage. But it has since been forgotten, and the current official position is to ignore the phenomenon entirely, since the authorities have proven themselves unable to control it anyway.

It is not hard to find people who will discuss their experiences, but the descriptions, even from those individuals with observational training, are unsatisfying. No two reports are alike, rarely even similar. Experiences are so clearly subjective that nothing definitive can be surmised.

Some pilgrims claim that they have physically, verbally asked questions of the cat, and verbally received replies, in whatever language they happen to know or to use. Others report what can only be described as some kind of direct rapport or mind-to-mind contact; they feel that they have been radically changed, but are unable to explain exactly what is different. Still others allude to some kind of purely mystical experience that they do not even attempt to put into words. Almost everyone feels that they have had some kind of personal interaction with the cat.

There are numerous works of art whose inspiration is attributed to Al Shagat. After visiting Al Shagat, the painter Andrej Pelidor spent the last eight years of his life painting canvas after canvas in shades of blue that few could even distinguish; whether he ever succeeded in achieving the hue that he desired will never be known.   Following her encounter with the cat, Countess Theodora Ishtar vaan Hohenheim started composing pieces based on what has since come to be known as 'fractal harmonies', but within a year suddenly turned her back on composing music altogether and took up weaving.

Beyond that, we have the cases of madness and death. None of the pilgrims seem to be greatly disturbed by such incidents. Perhaps they sense that it has in some way been worth it for the affected person. It does seem, at least, that someone amongst the crowds always takes care of the necessary arrangements for these unfortunate or — who can say? — blessed ones.

Viewed from afar, nothing much appears to be happening at the oracles of Al Shagat. The cat sits quietly on its dais — usually a rocky outcropping, a small plateau — and pilgrims gather in a semi-circle around it, encased in their life-support systems or in small, surface vehicles. A pilgrim may remain in the circle for hours or for days. Except for vehicles arriving and leaving, the scene appears rather static and unremarkable.

Now and then, at rather infrequent intervals, the ground begins to shake, the surface of the planet vibrates — Al Shagat is 'purring'. No other term could be possible here. It does not take a trained eye to see the rhythmic throbbing of that great furred throat. The eyes, barely visible beneath the thick lashes, seem to cast a new and strangely luminous light. When this takes place, there is in fact universal agreement afterwards as to what the onlookers are experiencing: *peace ... peace ... deepest peace ...*

Now and then someone comes to Al Shagat (no doubt there will never be an end to such people) with such questions as: Who are you? Where did you come from? What is your purpose here? Understandably they would like to have the mystery surrounding the creature and its origin cleared up. Perhaps they would like to find out if our theories concerning the Creators are correct, and expect this creature to be able to tell them. Needless to say, we cannot report any answers to you. Not because the cat refuses to reply; that is not it. It neither refuses nor complies with anything. Rather, the questioner never comes to asking the question. Perhaps, in the actual presence of Al Shagat, questions recede into insignificance. Maybe that in itself is proof that our minds do not behave in a reliable fashion in the presence of this phenomenon. Perhaps the ones who learn the answers to such questions are the ones who do not return. Or could it be that, in experiencing the mystery, we choose to let it remain forever mystery?

It might be considered surprising that there is no particular legend or cult surrounding the strange phenomenon of Al Shagat. The Special Investigator's Report summarizes our best guess as to the origin of the cat. The intent of this report is merely to document the presumed involvement of a Creator in order to further our scientific understanding of those entities. It thus limits itself to a simple physical description of the phenomenon, while totally avoiding speculation on the subjective experiences of the pilgrims. To this day, no other significant work on the subject has come forth.

What does exist in the folklore, in the folk consciousness, is a certain sense of gratitude that the cat is there at all. Even those who never have, or certainly never will make the pilgrimage, often feel a sense of comfort in the fact that someplace, even in an utterly inaccessible place halfway across the universe, there exists a seemingly transcendent being that could make a critical difference in their own small lives. Somehow, this feels like a consolation for the multitudes of potential pilgrims or just curious souls of our far-flung worlds.

The only realm of speculation in the folklore — or fantasy — surrounding Al Shagat concerns the creature's eschatology, its ultimate destiny. Will it die? (Usually considered impossible in any normal sense.) Will the Creators some day come back to whisk it away, or even reveal their plan for it? Will it someday simply disappear into the cosmos much as they appear to do? These questions give rise to speculation, certainly, but do not seem to be a cause for concern. The folk wisdom is that one day Al Shagat will indeed disappear, will in some fashion cease to exist for us, come to an effective end. Perhaps there is a hint of sadness or loss inherent in this belief, but in a larger sense, the creature's destiny seems to be not only out of our hands but, in the end, immaterial.

Even when it is gone, it will still exert its influence, and so in a sense, it will never end. Merely having existed once, it will exist forever. So even if we no longer have the present mystery of its existence, we will have for all time to come the reminder of Mystery, and that, perhaps, is ultimately its gift to us.

The Library at Antagua

The Library at Antagua is neither very large nor exceedingly ancient, but it has its own curious history and traditions which are well worth retelling.

The Library sits high up on the slopes of Monzi Perpigno. Below it stretches the beautiful and fertile plains of Tellares l'Veixi with the river snaking through the middle of it on its way to the deep blue bay. Above the Library is the handsome abbey of Antagua, which dates back to the second or third century, and which has supplied the Library with most of its Librarians.

The Library is now some six hundred and sixty years old. The original collection of books was donated by Pjodr Alexis Luc Agustin, the first Landgraaf of Tellares and the builder of the first dike system on the L'lares. He bequeathed his personal library to the abbey on the condition that the monks provide it with a suitable home. They did so, completing the first Library building in less than a year, a lovely and sturdy edifice of rough-hewn stone provided with magnificent windows facing North, East, and South, which give a commanding view of the plains, the bay, and the wild, wooded country to the South.

This is the preferred reading room to this day, although the Library has changed substantially in the intervening centuries. The first building was barely large enough for the

original collection, and as the collection grew, under the tutelage of a dynasty of Librarians, to many times its original
size, rooms were added in a rather haphazard manner over
the centuries, ranging up and down and around the sides of
the mountain, and connected by a maze of walkways and
stairs.

Although the Library was first donated to the abbey, the
Library today is under the protection but no longer under the
control of the abbey. Nominally subject to the authority of
the abbot, the head Librarian today enjoys a prestige and
independence that is in fact comparable to that of the abbot
himself. This is in large measure due to the efforts of the
Third Librarian, Ifrenza, a man of indomitable character and
enduring influence, who first became Librarian and only
later abbot. To this day he remains the only person to have
occupied both high offices simultaneously.

The organization of the Library is one of its more curious
aspects. Whereas most libraries, even much smaller ones,
will have their books arranged according to some set of cate-
gories or other (or, on occasion, chronologically), the Library
at Antagua would appear at first glance to be arranged in a
totally haphazard fashion. And this may, in fact, be the most
accurate description of its curious arrangement.

This 'random' ordering may have derived originally
from the collection of Landgraaf Pjodr, however, it was for-
malized and institutionalized by the Third Librarian himself.
There are certainly patterns in the arrangement of books in
the Library, but the underlying principle seems to be that this
pattern can change month by month, sometimes even day by
day, and is subject solely to the design — some would say
whim — of the Head Librarian. While any reader may freely
remove and set aside books from the shelves, it is the personal prerogative of the Head Librarian alone to replace
them. And lamentably the Librarian's efforts at restoring

order often prove to be vexatious for the ordinary scholars who use the Library.

So it is that a monk or a scholar who has been coming to the Library for weeks perhaps, will one day, without any warning, find the set of books that he or she has been studying, summarily scattered, unexpectedly rearranged about a dozen different places throughout the Library, quite likely among different rooms.

This is probably not due to any particular intent, but most likely simply a result of the Librarian having stumbled across them, having 'borrowed' most of them to read himself, then having returned them one by one to arbitrary but seemingly appropriate places on the shelves.

There may indeed appear to be whole sections of the collection that are broadly dedicated to particular topics, but this is oftentimes deceiving. The very book that one is looking for may have been put back amongst those of some other, patently unrelated subject. This may well be intentional, but one cannot avoid the suspicion that it is more likely the product of inattention.

If one wishes to locate a particular book or subject matter expeditiously, it is best to make a request of the Head Librarian himself; otherwise, a search could last for hours or even days. If he is not busy, he will most likely be able to walk directly to the proper shelf and lay his hand on the desired volume immediately, although it is not uncommon for even the Librarian to lose track of books (only temporarily, to be sure). In such cases, the best he may be able to do is to refer the reader to various shelves or rooms where a search is likely to be most fruitful. The Librarian may sometimes help one pursue the search but only until he himself finds some interesting book and opens it up to read. Or until the next reader approaches him with a request.

The Librarian's primary duty is to become familiar with

all of the books of the Library, in order to better be able to
locate information when it is called for. Related to this is the
neverending task of arranging the books in a seemingly more
useful or more illuminating way.   Unlike some other
libraries, there is no index or catalog enumerating the books
of the collection, so it is solely the memory and knowledge of
the Librarian that is responsible for maintaining order.

But what kind of order varies from Librarian to
Librarian, from year to year, even from day to day. They say
that the Third Librarian and some of his successors had read
and were familiar with every single volume in the entire collection, and that they could even readily leaf through a book
to find the pages that contained a sought-after reference.

That may have been possible in the days when the
Library was much smaller, but it is surely not realistic to
expect any more. Today, our Librarians may have read many
books indeed, compared to the rest of us, but oftentimes the
best they can expect is to fleetingly skim over most of the
books, familiarizing themselves generally with their contents, even if only superficially and perhaps temporarily.

Our present Head Librarian is named Morphius He is
quite an elderly man, some even say senile, and lame in the
bargain. What is certain is that he sleeps a lot, sitting behind
the desk in his little alcove in the darkest, westernmost corner, with books piled around him. When addressed, he is
laconic to the point of muteness, often just shuffling away
silently to the proper place among the shelves, proffering the
desired book absentmindedly to the petitioner, already distracted by some new title that catches his eye.

Yes, he certainly seems learned enough, our Morphius,
but there are some concerns about the succession after he is
gone. He has three assistants, but they are much younger
men than he, one of them hardly more than a youth. They all
seem cut from the same cloth: lean, ascetic men, clean-

shaven, with high foreheads and closely-cropped dark hair, silent as Morphius himself, utterly devoted to their books. All three wear eyeglasses.

But their devotion is of a sort that may prove in the end to be of little value to other readers. Perhaps they are all too absorbed in their books. When Morphius is asleep or not to be found, it is to one of these young men that we must turn. Each has his own desk, piled high with books, buried in separate corners of the Library. But it is difficult to get their attention. When one does finally look up from his reading, his eyes seems lost in far-away realms, and it may take long moments for them to come to focus on the person who is standing right in front of him. And the question will invariably be met with a blank-faced stare. More often than not, one is tempted to repeat the question, perhaps more loudly or deliberately. This may produce in turn a frown of deep concentration. Evidently it takes a great effort for the young librarian to detach himself from his inner world in order to attend to the matter at hand.

They are certainly dedicated and learned enough; once the question has sunk in, the young librarian will get to his feet (silently, to be sure) and lead the way through the timeless passages. And then he will stop and pull a book from the shelves and begin to examine it. But most likely this has nothing whatever to do with the book that was requested; the fellow has merely been distracted, and one must get his attention all over again, and even repeat the question if one wishes any assistance at all ...

So you see, as learned as they may be, these young men are not of great use to those who come to use the Library. Morphius we can deal with; as silent and as slow as he is, he attends to our needs, finds what is requested before sinking back into his own realms. But these young assistants of his, they grow more abstracted with each passing year, they seem to fade ineluctably into the very stuff of thought itself. Already one hesitates to approach them except as a last resort. Yet it has always been the prerogative of the Head Librarian to appoint his successor, and thus far no other likely candidates have appeared on the scene but these three. Perhaps, if one of them is chosen, readers in the Library will indeed be entirely on their own. Perhaps then the organization of the Library will indeed become random, that is to say, chaotic.

But if that does happen, it may be a blessing in disguise. Doubtless any of these assistants would be too absorbed in his own affairs and be too detached from the needs of the outer world to appoint or train assistants to succeed him. Thus in another fifty years or so — one may imagine by then that the Library would be just a succession of piles scattered about the shelves and on the floors — in fifty years the custody of the Library would revert back to the abbey, which could then choose either to close it entirely, or to appoint someone entirely new to take charge of it. Perhaps this time it should be someone who has little interest in learning itself, but who enjoys organizing and taking care of things for their own sake. Perhaps a bookkeeper or a miller would be a good choice.

In the meantime, the Library is open every day, from dawn to sundown, except for the religious holidays, and its magnificent view should make it a favorite destination for an afternoon's outing. Yet surprisingly, few choose to come here merely to enjoy the scenery. The three magnificent windows of the old Library building provide an incomparable view of the land and the sea, but those who inhabit the desks within show little interest in mere physical landscapes.

That is the Library at Antagua.

Dreams of Sand

The great cattle-god, Har-en-no-pe, arrived in our city last week, a gift to our prince from 'Li-Tekbal, crown prince of Assady and Muuer, the great green kingdom of the West, which lies far beyond the western Deserts, at the outermost edge of the Earth.

The caravan bearing the god arrived during the night of 'Hak-neh, in the last phase of the moon of the roaring winds, at the gates of our city. And there it had to wait, like all caravans, for the purification rites, as well as to fulfill the laws of passage. And if the god was impatient, waiting a day and a night as it did, it did not show it. But who knows if a cattle-god has any power over our desert realms, and what use do we have for a cattle-god anyway?

The god's image was a gift, so we accepted it and inscribed it into our temple. But not before every person and animal and article in the caravan had been inspected and registered and granted admittance into the city, according to the provisions of the ancient laws. And of course, every living creature had to be purified by being dusted with sand and having the Great Chant sung over their heads by a young child, as they prostrated themselves in the sand: "Liiiuhkbehnah — Samsarseeeht — Hahrnileeehsna — Patnahsoiii" "The Sand, in its infinite bounty, grants you a few moments." Naturally, it took three or four strong men to hold down some of the animals for this necessary rite.

As mentioned, there was no great interest in the cattle-god itself, but we accepted it, as we accept all gifts and all torments. After all, if the Desert allows anyone to pass through its midst, it can only be because it chooses to let them pass. So all visitors are, truly seen, messengers of the Sands, even though they themselves may know nothing of their mission. How many of us in this city, in fact, actually believe in the distant lands and realms that these pilgrims rave about? Oh, it is true, we enjoy listening to them, and exchange tales with them, and trade our goods for theirs, but for most of us, no doubt, this is but a faintly concealed masquerade. For we know that no sooner shall they pass out of sight of our city walls again, than they shall fade and dissolve once more into the Sands from which they sprang.

In the distant past, a number of foolish young men have attempted to journey to these far-away lands, and we even have stories of a few who have claimed to return, bearing tales of fantastic countries beyond the edge of the Infinite Desert. But that is only to be expected. Certainly, the Great Desert, Father and Mother of all life and all death, can perform such trivial miracles as these, just as it sends the sun to rise daily from the Sands of the East, and to set again in the Sands of the West.

But the true meaning of the tales these strangers bear, the hidden messages of the Desert buried beneath or interwoven with their seemingly casual reports of supposed distant lands and people — these are the subject of endless speculation and study amongst our populace, and we long ago established and amply endowed a priestly caste to direct and record these studies for us. There are, of course, many among us who refuse to see any meanings hidden in these outlanders' words, who hold that all is simply a fabrication of the Desert, intended to amuse us or perhaps to confuse us.

And naturally, there are always a few who accept these accounts at their face value, who claim that these visitors are as real as you and I (which is undeniable) and that the Desert has in fact created cities much like ours, even greater than ours, peopled with men and women whose existences are just as vital to its plan as ours are ...

We cannot prove that there is no truth in these claims, but can only point out that most of us, most of the time, laugh at them. How much simpler it is to believe that ours is the central creation of the Infinite Desert, that each caravan that arrives from afar has been conjured up solely as a gift or a punishment for us, and that after it departs from our city it will be swallowed up once more by the dunes. How much simpler, and also, how much richer! For if this most widely held belief be true, then every word uttered by every one of these strangers in our presence is in truth a message directly from the very Desert itself, from the same source as ourselves and all creation, and the ramifications of each word are thus Infinite and inscrutable. And this does seem to be the case. For no matter how one looks at any object that any of the caravans brings, no matter how one interprets any sentence that any visitor utters, there always seem to be more and greater meanings and realities beyond them, sometimes only dimly glimpsed, at other times perceived with piercing clarity.

But most of the time we lead out lives without being aware of the ground of our beings, and presumably this, too, is the plan of the Desert. We go about our work, dig up our food and the things we use out of the Sand, beget and bear children, drink our wine and sing our songs. At night we may cry out in pain, in the middle of the day we are wont to dance and laugh. Our priests, supposedly, are above these lowly pursuits, brood for hours on end on the Desert's mysteries, and occasionally uncover some previously unsuspected truth or conjecture. We listen to them with serious faces, then laugh at them as soon as they walk away. We continue to provide for them, not because we value their revelations, but simply because it is our way, just as it is our way to provide for our children.

Occasionally one of our citizens will ascend the high walls surrounding our city — when these walls were built, no one can ever hope to discover — and look down at the surrounding Desert for minutes or for days. Usually all is still, but sometimes a drama unfolds itself in the distance or nearby the walls ... A trick of the Sands, or is it really happening? We do not know; we can only say what we see and go on. If the Desert wished us to know, it would surely tells us, so it can only be its will that we continue blindly.

The Rock People
and the Hill People

It is said — in another, distant country — that the Rock People and the Hill People are always there waiting. Who ever saw one moving? And yet they do. Everyone knows of a pile of rocks at the base of some cliff that obviously came down from that cliff, though always it was long before anyone's memory. But when my grandfather was a young man there was a whole village buried beneath a pile of rocks, up in the Barent Mountains. One moment everyone heard this huge, roaring noise — twenty miles away it was heard, at least — the next moment they were all gone, buried beneath a sea of huge boulders that filled the valley from end to end. A few people were out of the way and somehow survived, but having seen the destruction and having lost everything and everyone ... I wonder, how many would rather have died with the rest?

So the Rock People do sometimes move quickly, though presumably they spent years and years and years deliberating amongst themselves, until one morning, finally, they were all ready, the last thought in that regard had been uttered, the last question answered, and then — what power could stop them?

We know they are unbelievably ancient, and many would claim that their thoughts move no quicker than the seasons pass upon the land. But I and others dispute this. I believe that if you go someplace where there is no sound from people or animals, and wait quietly until even the wind stops blowing for a moment, and if you let your ears listen at the center of this quietness, I believe that the low, roaring sound you will hear are the thoughts of the Rock People. And they are so quick and so subtle that you can not even understand one of them; all that you can hear is the thousands and thousands and thousands of them together, like one huge voice, and this voice filling the earth and the sky, so that we do not even recognize it unless we stop everything and listen.

And the wind, some others say, are but the Great Voice of the Rock People of One Place, calling to the Rock People of the Other Places, and it goes from place to place on the earth, bearing their news and their secrets. And it is said, whoever listens to the wind will become wise. So this is why.

Do they know anything about us at all, these So-Ancient-Ones, these That-Move-So-Slowly? Do they have any regard for our Human Race of People? One would hardly think so, seeing how a thousand and thousand of them might move upon a village in just a moment, wiping out everything. Did they maliciously plan our destruction? Did they not even care, maybe not even realize we were there? Did they perhaps even foresee the harm and move forward regretfully, though resolutely, accepting the necessity while mourning the loss? How can we ever know? Their thoughts — if that is what the wind and the voice within the silence bears — their thoughts are beyond us, mere human beings. They came before us, came before all the animals and birds and fish and plants. Who knows, perhaps they preceded the rains and the snows. After the last man has died, the Rocks will hold his wake and then bury his body. That we bury our bodies in the earth is but a fatuousness of our foolish minds.

For it is the Rock People and the Hill People that truly bury them, that take back their substance, which we have only borrowed.

We do indeed gather up these Seemingly-Meek-Ones and with our chisels and hammers break them up into shapes more useful to us, and erect walls and houses, and occasionally castles and palaces. And they seemingly comply with our wishes, submit meekly, do not seek to escape. For they know, as we do, that our walls will collapse, our houses fall and crumble, even the grandest palaces our race has made will one day pass back to their tribe. For they have lent us their bodies, and they will reclaim them when we are done, just as they reclaim our own used up bodies.

For we are their children, and they our ancestors. It was out of the Earth, out of the Rock World, that we sprang up, generations ago beyond memory, along with the first animals and birds and fishes and plants. If anyone could understand the winds, he might understand their secrets and know why. But even if one person were to spend all the years of his life listening, what would he have but the most paltry cupful of their thoughts, which fill up the World like an endless sea, stretching boundlessly in all directions, and far beyond any memory into times past and into times to come ...

The Greatest Show

Among the Beasts

The trainer came out to train the beasts.

First there was the lion. He was in a foul mood. There was an infection on his paw that no one knew about and that was causing him grief. Usually a minor nuisance, the flies were hounding him unmercifully today, alighting on all of the most sensitive surfaces, as if purposely tormenting him. Finally, the meat that had been thrown to him was spoiled, and no one knew or cared. He had picked at it on and off throughout the morning, driven as much by boredom and discomfort as by hunger. Occasionally he might find some spot where the meat was more or less edible, and chew on it for a few minutes before the unpleasant taste prevailed and caused him to spit it out.

The lion's name, absurdly, was Felix.

The trainer's name was Desmond DuMonde. He was 41 years old and an alcoholic. He had actually been born Randall Douglas Blouncher, but had changed his name at the age of 22, when he had joined the Carnival Carioca, which was later absorbed by the Grand Circus Piccoli.

Desmond DuMonde knew that he was a failure in most of the things that mattered in life. He had two sons that he had not seen in eight or nine years. His last wife had left him two months ago, sick of the routine beatings. Not even Artemis the Fat Lady would lend him money anymore. He was given of late to sudden and uncontrollable bursts of rage which were causing him difficulties with the rest of the troupe. He did not know it, but he was actually very close to being let go in favor of his 24-year-old *protégé*. Only the unnoticed compassion of the assistant manager, Mike Defoe had allowed him to stay on. Defoe argued, cajoled, pleaded with Desmond to mend his ways, which even by the lax standards of this company were atrocious. He, Defoe, had finally decided that if there was one more outburst, Desmond would have to go. His young understudy, Martin, was still inexperienced, but seemed like he could rise to the occasion in a pinch. And what was more relevant at the moment, he was a modest, tractable, generally well-mannered young man, with nothing of the streak of meanness that sometimes possessed Desmond.

Desmond's one claim to success, his one area of competence and achievement was that he was a superb animal trainer. He had been doing it for almost twenty years and his skill was ingrained, almost impeccable. He could even carry off a decent show when he was drunk, and he had actually done so on numerous occasions. The rest of the company had gotten used to such spectacles; however Mike Defoe, when he came on three years ago, had put a stop to this practice, on the grounds that it endangered both the animals and the customers. Once he had even physically prevented Desmond from entering the ring. He had actually knocked him out and had him brought back to his trailer by the Strong Man. Defoe, small and wiry and eight inches shorter than Desmond, was an ex-boxer. He rarely displayed his anger nor used his boxing skill, but when he knitted his brow in a certain way, the others steered clear of him and he got his way.

Some trainers succeed by dint of extraordinary empathy for their animals. They spend hours just being with their animals, seeing to their comfort, grooming them, nursing them through illness or injury, bringing them special foods. This is often not done as a means to an end, but is simply a reflection of their interest, compassion, or simply love. The whip or whatever devices might be used in training and performances is really only a prop, a prompt. Their success lies in their keen sensitivity to the beasts' instincts and moods, and in the bond between trainer and animal.

Desmond was not of this particular school. His technique was purely that of dominance, which he established immediately with any new animal, and never relaxed. This was nowhere so clearly to be seen as when any new dog showed up at the circus grounds, whether it was someone's new pet or just a local stray. Within minutes, Desmond had the dog under his control, and he never gave an inch.

As a rule, Desmond was not cruel. He was a cool pragmatist, an "animal realist" as he styled himself. He understood intimately each animal's capabilities as well as its limitations. Certainly he had a working knowledge of each species' psychology. Above all, he knew its fears.

He used whips, poles, sticks, prods as tools, nothing more. The beasts he trained were the medium he manipulated, and he worked them as coolly and as skillfully as an expert woodcarver might shape a piece of wood. He was concerned about their health or well-being only insofar as it affected their performance; he left it to others to provide the care and the nurture.

Occasionally, Desmond could become cruel. It usually happened in the heat of practice, when everything was going his way. At those times, when the animal and he were both performing the most superbly, when everything was working right and both he and the beast were at their peak, at those times he would sometimes push harder than he had a need to, than perhaps he should have. And then he would not tolerate any resistance on the part of the animal. Snarls would be answered with sharper blows, a refusal to cooperate entirely might elicit an angry beating. Sometimes the animal might be bullied into complying, and actually carry out a feat that neither he nor it had imagined possible. Sometimes it might balk and just endure a beating. Any attempt to fight back would be answered by unrestrained brutality. Occasionally an unfortunate animal would be left bruised and bloodied and unable to work for some time afterwards. Desmond had the sense then to let it be for a while; his outbursts ended when the animal was clearly defeated, and the next day he was once more a realist.

This morning Desmond DuMonde was not drunk. He had been drinking heavily the night before, but now he was freshly rested, had a full stomach and had even showered for the first time in a week. Nonetheless, he wore the same filthy and shabby clothes that he had been working in for days. His hairy belly protruded grossly from the grimy tee shirt. He had started the day feeling generally in a good mood, although now there was something unpleasant gnawing at the edge of his consciousness.

After his last talk with Mike Defoe, Desmond had finally realized that even as skillful as he was as a trainer, his days with the company might be numbered. But rather than considering what he could do to mollify his boss, let alone mend his ways, he was chewing over all the things that he imagined were wrong with his assistant Martin, the one who would surely replace him if he were fired. He imagined that not only did Martin look at him with a certain derision these days, but that he was secretly scheming to take Desmond's job away from him. All of Martin's already considerable skill and innate talent Desmond now saw as mostly dumb luck and pretentiousness. ... The little turd! Desmond spat angrily onto the ground.

So by the time he walked into the lion's area, he was

decidedly sullen and angry.

The lion noticed Desmond enter, but he was too distracted by his own troubles to pay him very much heed. His paw was throbbing. Desmond took the lion's indifference as an affront. As mentioned, he usually only became cruel in the heat of battle, but something turned differently in him today, and, uncharacteristically, he saw the lion as his personal adversary.

The lion and he knew each other very well. The lion was nine years old and had come to the circus as a youngster. He was now middle-aged, and for the most part he was a tractable, reasonably well fit, and dependable lion. He was not particularly curious or sociable, and was perhaps even a bit dull for a lion. Generally speaking, he was slow to anger.

Desmond answered the lion's indifference to his arrival with a crack of the whip against the ground that sent dust into the lion's eyes. The lion blinked and instinctively snarled and was rewarded with a stinging blow in the face. He responded, foolishly, by snarling again and batting futilely with his paw. This, of course, only spurred Desmond on; he next hit the lion on his hindquarters to try to get him onto his feet. The lion looked at him dully; the various discomforts of his body dulled his leonian brain. The sting of the whip and the relentless pain in his paw were the same. Desmond and the flies buzzed around him, harassed him. The taste of rotten meat still lingered in his mouth, while his stomach rumbled with hunger.

Desmond's mouth was distorted. He rarely uttered any words when working with animals. He was usually totally involved in what he was doing; the verbal part of his mind was simply absent. But today he spoke words, seemingly directed at the lion. What he said was: "You little turd!" Just three words, a mere moment of inattention. But it was a moment in which he was distracted, not entirely present.

The lion sprang. There was no clear intent to his action. If he could have expected anything at all, it would have been to be struck again, to be slapped back. He was merely responding to all of the insults that the world had been heaping on him for hours and for days.

Desmond was surprised. He was surprised to find himself falling backwards. It had never happened before. He was surprised at the incredible force of the lion's body slamming against his own. He was surprised to see the lion's face and jaws right next to his. He was surprised at the pain, sudden, blinding, rending. He kept commanding and expecting his arm to move, his whip to crack, but something was wrong; the whip had fallen from his hand. His last sensation was the incredible stench of the lion's breath.

Thomas Three-Arms Speaks

My name was Thomas Zook. Thomas Phillip Emmanuel Zook. For the last sixty years it's been Thomas Three-Arms. It's been so long since I've used the other name that I actually forgot what it was, and had to look back through my papers just the other day to remember all those other names.

My father, Matthias Zook, was a Heborite farmer in what was once the State of Iowa. Now it's called Upper Missouri Lowlands or some such thing, but for me it will always be Iowa. I was born about the time of one of those big wars that they used to have occasionally back then, where half of the world's nations were pitted against the other half. Actually, most of the people in those days couldn't have told you what the war was about or why they were fighting on one side and not the other; all they knew for sure was that their side was right and that the other side slaughtered babies or some such awful thing.

I remember my father as being huge, with a large, red face fringed with greyish-brown beard, and all dressed in black. I would have been afraid of him, except that he always seemed to be afraid of something himself, and it's kind of hard being very afraid of someone who's always afraid himself. What he was afraid of was God, who I always imagined to be an even huger man, about twice as big as my father, with an even longer, whiter beard, and dressed all in white rather than black. I always imagined that God could sort of pick my father up in one hand and toss him right through the air, right over the barnyard fence, say, and into a pile of cow-shit.

My mother, on the other hand, was afraid of my father. She was about the same general shape and color as him but a lot smaller, didn't even come up to his shoulders. She wasn't afraid of him hitting her, for I can't remember ever seeing my father actually strike anyone, but she sure seemed to be afraid of his voice. It was a loud voice, for sure, and whenever he got angry, which was fairly often, it was loud enough and hot enough to send anyone around scurrying for cover. God's voice I always imagined to be sort of like a thunderstorm, only much worse, because there was no place you could hide or be safe from it.

My mother was a kind of frightened person to begin with, and whenever my father started booming his voice around, she would start shaking, and get real silent and humble. I think maybe she saw my father as God's appointed representative on the earth. And I've often wondered whether she married him because she was afraid not to.

My father sold me off when I was thirteen. That's what I'd have to call it, though I'm sure that's not how he saw it. I was the middle one of five boys. There were no girls in the family. Later, I wondered whether my father and my mother slept together exactly five times in their life; it's hard to imagine even that much, but there's the five of us to account for. And we were spaced out about five years apart, so neither my older nor my younger brothers were much in the way of playmates for me. Not that any of us had much time for playing anyway. Farming in those times was hard work, or at least my father thought it was supposed to be. I think maybe he thought that God was always watching him and might start yelling at him if he tried to slow down and have some fun.

Now, my father used to think that I had been sent to him by the devil to punish him for his sins. He actually said as much in my presence. Sometimes I think he used to believe I was the devil himself, or maybe the devil's son. Maybe the reason I was never really afraid of him like everyone else in the family is that he was sort of afraid of me, being something from the devil. He never said that to me directly, but I picked it up from things I overheard, and by the time I was four or five I pretty much knew how things stood between us. So I'd obey him, like my brothers and my mother, but I didn't do it because I was afraid of him, just because he happened to be bigger than me and in charge of me for the time being.

I always wondered what my father's sins were that I was the punishment for. I never saw that he had much time or interest for doing the things that he considered sinful, so I guess they must have been sins in his heart — he believed that just thinking about doing something was exactly the same, in the eyes of God, as actually doing it. So I suppose that all the time he was running about and working and shouting at us and so forth, he was thinking all the while about sinful things that he wanted to do. And that's why he got sent me, he must have thought.

I don't mind his having gotten rid of me; in fact, I'm quite thankful for it. And I'm sure it did a world of good for him, too. I was just this three-armed, three-legged thing from the devil, and as long as I was around it was a reminder that God was keeping track of his sins and punishing him, and maybe cooking up something really awful for him later. So when I was gone it must have been a real relief and a burden off his heart. In fact, while all my brothers went to school at least some of the time, I was kept home. The reason I was kept home, of course, is that my father didn't want all our neighbors to all the time be seeing God's punishment on him and consequently be thinking about all the sins in his heart. That's not what he said, but that's why it was. What he said was that I was an idiot who couldn't hardly speak, let alone go to school and learn anything from it. It wasn't that I couldn't speak, I just wasn't much interested in speaking with most of the people around me, most of the time. But I spoke lots to my younger brother Ishmael, and he knew I wasn't an idiot at all, and my father did too. But in keeping me at home, it meant that he had to be seeing me all the time and be reminded of his sins. Thinking back on it, it seems to me my father would have been better off altogether if he hadn't kept me at home so much.

But he made me work, so I guess that was his compensation for having to look at me. I worked hard. I was strong and smart, and I liked to work, mainly because it meant that I could get away from him. I started doing things on my own when I was not even seven. He would just tell me what he wanted done, and I would just do it by myself, without much extra help or directions from him. Sometimes he would take me with him and let me learn new things, but usually I would just be watching while he showed one of my brothers something, like shoeing a horse, or how to saw fancy joints in wood, and I would just pick up on it and teach myself to do it without much help. He knew this and took full advantage of it, and that's why I say he knew I was no idiot. He just let on to other folks that I was, so that he wouldn't need to talk about me more.

So here I am, thirteen years old, never been to school in my life and can't read or write a tick, but I can do everything that needs be done to keep a farm running, wrestle cattle, splice rope, do carpentry, you name it. I'm not real big, but I'm strong. People don't say I'm strong, like they do about other boys, but they know it. From the work they have me do, you can see they know it.

So this man Richard Butcher starts coming around the place. He and my father are doing some business deals together. My mother and brothers make these cheeses, big, round, yellow wheels forty, fifty pounds — good, hard, tasty cheese. Mr. Butcher is selling them for him, fetching him a good price, selling them to some merchant over in Waterloo. My father calls Mr. Butcher 'English', which is what he calls everyone who isn't a Heborite. Mr. Butcher is a big man too, even bigger and rounder than my father, but somewhat younger, and real jolly. I'd never seen a butcher before, so ever since then, whenever I think of a butcher, I see the picture of Mr. Butcher as he was then; he's my idea of what a butcher should look like. Of course, he wasn't a butcher at all, although he sometimes dealt in meats. He was what we called a wheeler-and-dealer, a trader. Actually, I guess he did something of everything in his life, which wasn't real long, but what he was best at was making deals. He was always watching for where he could make a good deal, and it seemed there was no deal that could go by that he wouldn't see some way to get something out of it for himself, too.

Mr. Butcher is now long dead. He drank himself to death before he was forty-five, after his biggest deal fell through and left him with nothing but debts that he could never have paid off. He was a Baptist man, so he must have been afraid of God, too, but to see him laugh you never would have guessed it. He laughed a lot. It used to bother me for a long time when he would laugh at me. I thought he was making fun of me, which he was, but later I saw it was OK — that was just his way; he made fun of everything and everyone, including himself. This didn't stop him from drinking himself to death, though.

So my father and Mr. B, Richard Butcher, are doing these deals together, selling cheeses, and my father is pretty satisfied with the prices Mr. B is giving him. So Mr. B is visiting our place fairly often, so of course he notices me. He's heard of me before, but he's never seen me 'til now, so of course he figures I'm an idiot like they tell him. But when he starts coming around our place and sees me working, and talks to me, and sort of likes me, in spite of my three legs and three arms and my not saying much. He tells me jokes, which I think are stupid, and he gives me nicknames like 'Hot Shot', which I don't like at all, but still I like Mr. B somehow. His jolliness, next to my father's being angry and afraid all the time, is like fresh air. And a couple of times I get to go with Mr. B to the various farms around and help him out loading cheeses and other goods. And he sees that I'm strong and smart and that I make use of my third arm and leg to do things by myself that other people would need help with. So along about November of one year, when I'm just turning thirteen, Mr. B drives up to our place in his old black pick-up, and has a cup of tea and a chat with my father in the big parlor, just the two of them behind closed doors. I have the feeling that something important is going on between them, something important for me, so I manage to hang around the next room a lot while they're talking, and pick up some of their conversation.

What Mr. B is after, it comes out, is me. Once my father realizes this, I can hear that he's real happy to have the opportunity to get rid of me, and is careful not to bring up anything that might cause Mr. B to change his mind. In fact, he's so glad to be getting rid of me that I start feeling pretty mad at him; I would have expected him to be a bit more appreciative of my usefulness to him and at least think twice about it. But I guess the thing about God and the devil and the sins in his heart is a lot stronger, and every time he sees my three legs and three arms he's reminded of them again, so he's only too glad to send me off and forget that I was ever born.

Mr. B it seems to me, is trying not to sound too eager, even when he sees how eager my father is to be rid of me. So they have this real strange, kind of business-like conversation, and Mr. B says he wants to take me with him for three months to work for him, and that I'll be getting fifteen dollars a month plus board, and that he'll bring me back to the farm, if my father wants, come February or March. And my father says that's all just fine, and don't even bother to send me home from Webster City for Christmas, it's too far to be travelling just for that, and so forth.

Finally Mr. B gets up; the deal is finished and all he has to do now is fetch me, but at the last minute he decides, I think, that he is really getting too good a deal, and probably just to make himself feel a little better, he hands my father some money and says that it's an advance for my first month of work. My father is probably a little surprised by the sudden offering, and he takes it almost without acknowledgement, let alone thanks. Many years later, I learned, my father received fifteen dollars in exchange for me.

So that's how I was sold, and came to leave the farm where I was born, and to get out into the world. Like I said, I'm very grateful to my father for having sold me, for having given me the opportunity to escape. And I know that my leaving lightened his heart a good deal, and so I feel no bitterness at all, only thankfulness. What I wonder — what I'll never know — is whether my father saw my leaving as a sign that God had forgiven him and as the beginning of a new time of grace and bountifulness.

I was with Mr. B for almost four years, then I ran away. I ran away, in the end, because he didn't respect me. Because in spite of all his jolliness and good cheer, he treated me like his property, and sometimes he beat me. The first time he beat me was just three weeks after he bought me. It was because I couldn't read or write. He had assumed, I suppose, that because I was smart in other ways, I could read and write at least as well as any other thirteen year old. One day he asked me to copy down some figures into one of his account books, and when I told him I didn't know how, that I couldn't read or write, he got real mad and started slapping and kicking me around. I cried a lot too, not so much because it hurt, which it did, but mostly because I thought that Mr. B was my friend, and now he was treating me this terrible way. I just couldn't understand it. But things had not been going well with his business, and he had been drinking, and when I told him I didn't know how to write, he thought that I just didn't want to, and he just went crazy and started beating me. Later, he was real sorry, and he saw that I really didn't know how to read and write, and so he taught me. He was alright as a teacher, and I picked it up fast, but I never did really forgive him for beating me, even though he was drinking. I never could see that as an excuse for hitting someone.

And also when he drank a lot — but other times, too, when he was trying to make me work extra hard — he would start calling me names, and making fun of my extra arm and leg, not in the jolly way that he usually made fun of things and that I accepted, but in a way that really hurt, that made me feel like trash. I can remember many times — lying on my tiny bed and hearing him snore away in the next room — I can remember many times wanting to go to the kitchen and get the big butcher knife and slam it right into his big heaving butcher's belly, or right into his huge, mean, butcher's heart, and then watch the blood overflow the bed and form a big, big pool, dark red in the pale moonlight, widening and widening and widening ... There would be an awful lot of blood in such a big man.

But mostly I just contented myself with saying things behind his back, with cursing him inside my head. I think he probably suspected some of this, but didn't care, as long as I did as I was told. By the time I was sixteen, we had worked out a regular way of dealing with each other, kind of like what I had with my father: I would pretty much do what he wanted, efficiently and without complaint; he would be friendly and jolly on the surface, occasionally displaying some resentment or anger that I never understood. I sometimes almost loved him, but other times absolutely hated him and thought about killing him. The main difference between him and my father was that my father was always somewhat afraid of me, whereas Mr. B wasn't. His generosity and kindness were really just calculated to keep me dependent on him; and when he got drunk, his true feelings would often come out, and he would abuse me verbally and physically as well.

So I ran off. I stole ten dollars from him before I left, so I suppose he ended up cursing me thoroughly. Actually he had never once paid me or my father the fifteen dollars a month that he had promised my father, so I figured that this was only a drop in the bucket compared to what he owed me. The most that he had ever given me was twenty-five cents on two or three occasions.

I had been planning to run away for some time, and thought that I was ready to make my way on my own. I thought that I knew a lot about the world and that ten dollars was a lot of money. Wrong on both counts! Except for one afternoon in Waterloo, the biggest place I had ever been in was Webster City, the county seat. I didn't know anything; and ten dollars couldn't even get me half way to New Orleans, which is where I had decided to go, just by looking at it on a map.

But I knew I had to get as far away from Webster City as I could. I'd heard people talk about hopping freight trains, but had never tried it before myself. And being rather conspicuous, with my extra limbs, I decided that I would have to travel by night for the time being. So the first night I caught a freight train heading east. I knew that the great Mississippi River lay to the east, and that then I would have to go south, that I would pass through cities called Davenport, Saint Louis, Memphis, and finally New Orleans. Would my journey take a week, a month? I didn't know; I couldn't even guess.

It took me over three months, but then I didn't take a direct route. After a few days on the rails, I decided that I liked that life and would follow it for a while. My ten dollars had shrunk to only two, but I discovered a whole society that I had no inkling of before, and one which received me with open arms, despite my pennilessness and ragged clothing, despite my extra arm and leg, which had repulsed so many in the past.

I had many teachers, and I will not forget any of them. It was wintertime and cold, but those I met did not hesitate to share what warmth and shelter and food they had. I travelled across the continent several times, learned how to scrounge a good meal from a garbage can, when and how to best steal food, where to sleep soundly and securely at night, how to tell if a stranger meant ill or good. Even today, with nearly eighty years behind me and a comfortable life after an illustrious career in the circus, I sometimes feel a longing for the days when I was homeless and broke, but sheltered by the brotherhood of vagabonds. And more than once I have left my comfortable home overlooking the bay and gone wandering across the land, in my most ragged clothing and without a penny in my pocket. They know me still across the continent, though all the old-timers are dead now. I think sometimes, when I am ready to die, I will slip out of the city on a night freight train, so that I can die under the stars, among comrades.

Ah, but the circus, the circus! I did make it to New Orleans, finally, but three months had passed, more than three months. I was seventeen now; I was strong and quick, and actually becoming pretty cocky. I had figured out how to make a living on the road and liked it as well as anything I had known. And I would probably have gone on like that indefinitely, for years maybe if it hadn't been for a close brush with the law.

It was our own fault actually, me and a man named Harry Brewster McKnight. We should have known better than to sleep where we were, but the weather had suddenly turned bitterly cold again, and we just wanted some place warm for the rest of the night. It must have been long after midnight when they nabbed us. Someone must have seen us go into that warehouse, I can't figure it out otherwise that they'd be snooping around there at two in the morning. But there they were: flashlights, pistols, the works. Three of 'em, so there wasn't much thought in our minds of trying to run. They put handcuffs on Harry, but once they had a good look at me, all they could do was laugh like crazy and crack jokes, and they either forgot or didn't think handcuffs were necessary. There was this giant-sized man, about six foot six inches and weighing maybe three hundred pounds, who led me away by holding my third arm twisted painfully across my back.

Looking back, I don't suppose anything serious would have happened to us, a few days or weeks in jail maybe, but in my mind I saw myself being handed back to Mr. Butcher, or even to my father, and the thought of that frightened me even more than I can explain. I guess I had tasted a kind of freedom and a sense of self-esteem that I had only dreamed of before, and the thought of returning to that other world made me ill.

I don't know what moved Harry to do what he did.

Could he have had some inkling of what I was feeling? I am sure, at the least, that he got a beating for it. It's conceivable that he even paid with his life. Those were brutal days; it's hard for people nowadays to comprehend.

They had us out of the warehouse, and were marching us alongside the tracks, when Harry suddenly lurched away from the man who was leading him, kicked the flashlight out of the third man's hand, and smashed my captor firmly in the hip, so that I was set free.

"Beat it, kid! Run! Don't turn around!" His words were completely unnecessary. Though at other times it would have been inconceivable to desert a comrade in distress, it was not only Harry's clear desire to sacrifice himself, but there was nothing closer to my heart at that moment than escaping. So I ran. Though some people think I walk awkwardly, the third leg has never really hindered my movement, and that night, I can assure you, I really learned its true usefulness, I came to see it for the first time as a gift rather than a curse. Such a source of stability and security on invisible, rugged ground! I ran from my captors as I had never run before, I flew! I half expected a gunshot, but there was none; it was too dark; they had no idea where to shoot. Probably they did not even try to follow, but contented themselves with beating up Harry. Poor Harry! Years later, thirty years later, I tried looking for him, tried uncovering some news of his fate. But by then he was long dead, I am sure; he was maybe forty-five, fifty years old when he saved me.

The next night I hopped one of my last freights for a long time to come. I had decided that I never wanted to return to the world of Richard Butcher and Matthias Zook, that I'd better get away from the scene of my capture as quickly as possible and lay low for a while, seek out some different kind of living. So once more I set my sights for New Orleans, and this time I made it there, after three days of travelling.

I lived in the alleyways, out of trashcans for a few days, trying to figure out the city. It was a bigger one than I had ever lived in before, but that was all for the better. Bigger — more places to hide, more garbage, more stuff thrown away. But also — more people fighting among the garbage, more people to do you in.

After five days, I showed up early one morning at the union hiring hall, Longshoreman's Union, Port of New Orleans. I wanted a job as a longshoreman. They laughed me out of there. I was just seventeen, not very large, maybe a little skinny; looked weak, though I wasn't. Longshoreman? What's that funny thing hanging from your shoulder, kid? Why don't you leave your cane at home? You get run over by a train or something?

I left, lived among the garbage cans two more days, tried another place. Same result. I decided never to come back again; I spat on the floor of the hiring hall as I left. Back to the alleys. One day I met a black man on the street — back then they said 'colored man'. I told him about the union hiring hall. One day he took me with him to the Colored Longshoreman's Hall, walked in there with me, told them me and him were cousins and wanting a job together. That man's name was Louie Scarbo. They gave me some strange looks, but they took me on as a colored man, gave me some work, and for the first time in my life I was earning money for myself. I got myself a room in the Morrison Hotel and started going to bars with Louie, though I didn't much like the taste of drink. People still gave me plenty of trouble, on account of the extra limbs, but Louie stuck up for me, he told people we were cousins enough times that I think he finally started believing it himself. In fact, I started believing it.

But one day we're outside a tavern on the waterfront, and some sailor starts making jokes at me. He's pretty drunk and not really being nasty, just making fun like lots of people do, but Louie tells him to lay off, tells him we two come together and that if he bothers his pal, he better watch out for him, Louie.

I don't know what happened. The sailor just goes crazy. All of a sudden Louie is down on the sidewalk, bleeding; there's a knife in the sailor's hand. ... My friend Louie died on the sidewalk. I don't know what happened to the sailor, I was busy trying to take care of Louie. Then somebody came to take Louie off, and when I tried to follow, they pushed me away, said they would arrest me if I didn't get out of there.

I don't know what they did with him. I wandered around aimlessly. How long? Two days? Three? Sometimes I was crying and and talking to myself, sometimes I was just wandering about, not seeing anything. I didn't really sleep at all. Then, one morning, I lay down in the sun, on the grass in Jackson Park, in the old French Quarter, and took a nap. I was so tired, so tired ...

I don't think I was sleeping for long. Something hit against my foot. Then again. Someone was kicking my foot. I opened my eyes: a policeman — "No sleeping in the park!" In my confused state I was about to ask why, but before I could even open my mouth he gave me a contemptuous glare and walked off to bother someone else.

"No sleeping in the park!" "NO SLEEPING IN THE PARK!" The words echoed and echoed through my head as I stumbled out of there. "NO SLEEPING IN THE PARK!" It seemed a summary of all the world's petty rules and restrictions and prejudices. I didn't want to be in this world anymore, I decided; I would find my sleep in the river ... I wandered down the street, past shop windows, through crowds, not really noticing anything. I realized that I wasn't walking very straight, that I'd better be careful or they'd pick me up for drunk. And then I noticed a man: short, greying hair, dressed in a plain grey suit, a round grey hat on his head —

a bowler hat — face slightly pudgy, very cleanly shaven. I got the feeling that he was following me. I now remembered that he had been in the park. An undercover agent? I tried to shake him, decided that he really was following me, suddenly took fright and was about to dash across the street, make a run for it ...

"Excuse me. I'm in town with the Circus Mignese. I wonder if you might be interested in a job."

That man's name was Robert Butler. He brought me into the circus. It took a while for him to convince me that morning that he was telling the truth, that he really was with a circus. But that same day I went back with him to the fairgrounds, where the troupe was camped out, and that evening I had a hot meal amongst circus people and slept in a bed of my own. And when I awoke the next morning, inside a tent, I could not remember where I was, and when I remembered, I had to spend five minutes feeling the cot and the tent with my hands to convince myself that it was real.

Well, nearly sixty years have passed since that day, and almost fifty of those I spent with my family, the Circus Mignese, until it broke up, or I should say, was transformed into other things. I could have stayed on with one of the troupes that followed it, for my eyes are as sharp and my hands as quick as ever, but too many of my associates had died or retired from that world. Yes, it was quite a change, going from being a vagabond in the alleyways to becoming a performer in the circus, and eventually a star. Of course it didn't happen overnight — it took years of hard work, five years in fact, before I became well known.

But now I can think back on the days of my life and say that I'm content. I've seen enough wonders and heard enough applause to make up for all the Matthias Zooks, the Richard Butchers, the narrow-minded policemen with flashlights and manacles, who want to confine someone because they look different, or don't have enough money in their pocket, or a roof over their head. I count my relatives amongst the troupe of the Circus Mignese, now forgotten, many of them outcasts once: Nora — the Amazing Nora; the Dwarf Tribe; Sonia and Icarus, the flying stars of the flying trapeze; the Serpent Boy; Marcella the Magnificent; the Dancing Lalo; the Human Fish; and others, many others, nameless to you of the outside, but for those who lived that spectacle, never to be forgotten.

My friend and cousin Louie, you died for me, you spilt your red blood on the city streets. Harry Brewster McKnight, do you still roam the rails? Does your spirit? And I must thank you, Robert Butler, who saw my potential as a juggler long before anyone else. Did you already see it, that day in New Orleans, when you saw me lying on the grass in the city park, too grotesque a figure, with too many limbs to ever rest comfortably on ordinary grass, amongst ordinary men?

Icarus, the Flying Man

News of the death of the famous flying man reached us just the other day. Having known him intimately long before the world became aware of his strange powers, we were naturally saddened by his departure. While it is questionable whether he really had any friends or confidants, our long day-to-day acquaintance with the man certainly gave us insights lacking even in those scholars who reportedly devoted so many years to the superficial study of his physical body. Now that he is dead, I can see no possible harm in revealing that part of his story to which I am privy.

I should first explain who I am. For over forty years — until I retired three years ago — I was manager of personnel for a world-renowned circus troupe. One of my responsibilities was overseeing that group of performers that the vulgar public refers to as 'freaks'. I use that word with distaste even today. In those days I was known to become positively violent towards any outsider who uttered it in my presence — those within the company would never have stooped to such an insult. On the rare occasions when we needed to refer to these performers as a group, we always called them our 'specials'. Certainly their talents were of an inimitable nature. Among themselves they were known simply as the People.

Part of my job involved the recruitment and training of these special performers, and even more importantly, seeing that they remained happy and contented while they were with the circus. I know that there are many who claim that circuses and carnivals ruthlessly exploit these unfortunate humans for private gain, subjecting them to continual public ridicule and humiliation while throwing them a mere pittance to live on, then abandoning them in times of sickness and old age to suffer in isolation and despair. To my shame — to the shame of the world — I must admit that some of these claims are based on reality. Having lived in that world for decades, I have met many a man and woman who was cruelly used by others of our trade. Yet those of you who would despise us, I ask: How many of these poor creatures have *you* taken into your home? How many fed, clothed and educated? How many loved even as your own children? Yes, even those of the People who reported the cruelest treatments to me, even they admitted that their life in the circus was immeasurably better than anything they had ever experienced in the outside world. And though their lot was often a difficult one, they were never in a single instance prevented from leaving and seeking a better life elsewhere.

Though in other circuses stories of inhuman treatment of the People may have some basis in fact, I can personally confirm that in our own company that was never the case. Even before I entered the circus, our company, under the direction of the illustrious Alfonso Mignese, was known for its enlightened attitude towards these gifted individuals, and during my years their lot improved to the extent that the ordinary performers might well have complained about their privileged position, had not the People taken it upon themselves to extend their charity to their less fortunate associates ...

Once, disaster struck some far-flung relatives of one of our trapeze artists. Their house had burned down and a multitudinous family had travelled hundreds of miles to throw themselves upon the charity of their famous cousin. He, unfortunately, was virtually penniless, having squandered his ample earnings on women and horses. It was Magnus Magnussen, one of the dwarves, who provided the money to put up ten people for several months, and who went to great lengths to find them work, both in the circus and without. If he ever expected to be repaid, he never indicated it. When one of the prizewinning stallions was sick to death and about to be shot, it was Thomas Three-Arms who begged for a reprieve and then stayed with the horse for four days and nights, nursing it back to health. Nor was any of them ever too busy to watch the other performers' children while their parents practiced or took a trip to the city. And none was unwilling to work long hours repairing and maintaining the countless pieces of equipment that a great circus must have.

But if their kindness towards the other members of the company was remarkable, their devotion to their own kind was truly extraordinary. Hardly a city did we stop in that these genial beings did not pick up some deformed, unloved child or older person and bring them home to their 'colony', where the refugee was often miraculously transformed by the loving kindness of the People. Of course, not every person with a minor deformity or handicap has a place in the circus! To a large extent it was my onerous duty to determine which of them could remain with the troupe and which were merely guests. However, it is a testimony to the extraordinary good-will and resourcefulness of these gifted people that I never once had to suggest that they find another home for any of their wards. For those that could not be integrated into the circus, they quickly found other situations where the unfortunate person might have, if not affection, at least some respect and an honest living.

Often I am asked what it was like living among them. In all honesty, I must admit that one of the consequences has been that, after a number of years among the People, I came to view 'ordinary' people as being somehow deformed. They were lacking something. It was not merely the lacking of some extra physical organ, or the failure to stand out from the bland uniformity of their fellows, but the absence of some undescribable spiritual dimension that I came to expect from the People, and from some other rare individuals in the circus. So it was that after four decades I truly felt that I belonged to their family — for that is what it was — and when I finally retired from the circus, it was no surprise to any of us that three of my gifted colleagues chose to retire at the same time and to come live with me, not as servants, as some have disrespectfully suggested, but as honored companions.

But I digress from my story, the purpose of which is to relate the history of the flying man ... My account begins over thirty years ago; at the time we were travelling through the British Isles. I had been with the company then for upwards of ten years, and for the last several years in a responsible capacity. We had just finished our stand in a dreary industrial city and were preparing to leave. The crowds had been large, but somehow spiritless. Even the children here did not seem much given to laughter. This naturally affected our performance. A good circus becomes great only before an appreciative audience. After our last performance, I noticed a number of depressed-looking clowns milling about. This worried me as I knew that there were some problem drinkers in the company who were like to get soused just at such times as these. At the moment, though, I was much too busy to pay that observation much heed. We were scheduled to be moving again by the morning and I had work to do. I walked back to my trailer through the rain and began working out the payroll for the temporary helpers that we had hired from that area. The rain beat steadily against the roof of my quarters as I worked. It had been raining almost continuously during all of the six days that we had been here; perhaps that had something to do with the general lack of spirit.

I was quite immersed in my work when a brisk knocking at the door disturbed me. Peevishly I went to open up, thinking that it was likely a matter that could easily by handled without my assistance. My caller was a strong looking man with a well-creased face beneath a greasy, unkempt shock of brown hair. He wore the dirty, rather ragged clothes of a laborer. He was neither old nor young, but worn. His expression was a curious mixture of defiance and fearfulness. With him, I noticed, was Magnus, who barely reached to the man's waist. The stranger was just starting to speak, when Magnus quickly interjected: "I think this man has something important to tell you." Magnus' presence and obvious involvement tempered my unpleasant mood. I invited them in. The stranger explained that he had a boy — he avoided directly stating that it was his son — that he thought I might be interested in. The boy would be a good one for the circus, he thought. I glanced at Magnus, who nodded imperceptibly, signalling me that the child was one of his People. In my business the stranger's proposition was not an unusual one, although many of the unfortunate creatures that I saw were of little use for the circus. Nevertheless, the People did what they could for them, and that was often considerable.

We were scheduled to depart in a matter of hours, so it was imperative that I go to look at the child immediately, in spite of the lateness of the hour. I put on my coat again and stepped back out into the weather. The rain continued mercilessly.

To this day I could not tell you where we went. My mind was on other things and I simply followed Magnus and the stranger through the soggy, inhospitable night. Perhaps

Magnus knew something of the child's parents, but he is now fifteen years dead, and what he may have known died with him. So, other than the few scraps of information which I happened to recall and put down here, the origins of the flying man are completely unknown.

We came at length to a shabby house and entered. All I can remember about it is that it was tiny, poorly lit, and pervaded by an ill smell. A woman appeared from somewhere. Not only did she avoid looking at me directly, but she kept her face nearly hidden behind a scarf, as though she sought to hide her shame. She said something like: "So you've come to see the monster," and before I could even answer, she was leading the way into another room, separated from this one only by a rough curtain. This second room was even smaller and darker than the first. The man had to bring a lantern to show me what it contained. Lying there on a coarse, dirty mattress was what looked at first glance to be an unremarkable boy of perhaps five years, although one who was obviously extremely sick, perhaps dying. Except for a rag about the loins, he was naked. It was only as the man reached towards the child's arms that I noticed that their bone structure was not completely normal. There also appeared to be an excessive amount of fatty tissue along the boy's side.

As the man pulled out the boy's forearm, then unfolded a previously hidden limb from behind it, stretching the entire, triply-jointed arm straight out from the body, I began to realize the full extent of the boy's abnormality. And gasped. He had wings! Not the impractical sort of wings that humans ascribe to angels, but more like the wings of a bat. Where, in the normal human, the forearm narrows into a wrist, in this child it was considerably wider, and continued to form, not just into a hand, but also into a long, tapering extension of the forearm, which could either be extended out past the hand, or folded back behind the arm. Stretching between the elongated arm and the boy's body were thin membranes of skin, reaching at least to the hips. In those days, I thought that I had seen too many unusual human bodies to be much surprised by them anymore, but here for once I was truly astonished. I noticed that Magnus, who was looking on from behind us, was silently weeping. From his lips I made out the words he was uttering to himself: "Beautiful! Beautiful!" Quite correct, I thought, but also very ill, perhaps not long to live.

I don't really know what happened next. Somehow we got the boy out of there and back to the troupe. Magnus, foresightedly, had brought warm clothes to wrap him in. I was obliged to carry the child, who was too weak to walk more then a few steps. Somewhere during all of this, the man began demanding money. In my confusion, I wasn't able to understand what it was that he wanted, but I vaguely recall seeing some bank notes pass from Magnus to him. Later I learned that the gentle dwarf had paid the man fifty pounds from his own pocket, and he steadfastly refused to allow himself to be reimbursed from company funds. When I hear, as I sometimes do, some ignorant critic accusing our profession of trafficking in slaves, it is this transaction that always comes to mind. What more unjust accusation can be imagined? It was the world that had held this poor creature captive; we who had finally freed him from bondage.

The rest of that night I remember only dimly, carrying the boy into the trailer of Guida and Carla, who had obviously been expecting us; watching from a corner their skillful hands as they undressed him, carefully washed him, laid him in a clean bed, fed him from a bowl of hot soup. Sometime during all of this I must have fallen asleep, and it was then me whom these kind people led back to a warm bed and tucked away.

The boy Icarus quickly recovered. The name Icarus was

given him by the People, as he had no other. One of their first acts upon receiving a newcomer was to instill in them a hitherto unknown sense of pride or self-esteem. What had been seen by the world as a deformity they truly perceived as a unique mark of distinction or beauty, evoking not disgust, but admiration and affection. Being sincere, this feeling would quickly communicate itself to the new person, who had previously regarded themself as a monster. The resulting change in behavior was often sudden and dramatic. By naming the boy Icarus, the People immediately associated him with a tradition, ancient and proud. This was not done purposely, to achieve an end, but was rather the natural consequence of their native kindness and good humor.

Physically, Icarus improved immediately. Psychically, it was hard to tell. It may have been that he hadn't been so much mistreated at home as he'd been shunned, kept apart. Realizing that he had been born by some error into a completely alien world where he had no place and never would, where his life could have no fulfillment — realizing this, perhaps, he had simply chosen to die. Understand that this is all mere conjecture on my part. Perhaps he thought that he actually had died, and was now in a completely different world. Here he was, at least, recognized as a person, as a significant being, even though, as before, there was really no one capable of comprehending him fully. This new world, while not offering fulfillment either, at least did not exclude the possibility of it; it was worth continuing to live simply to explore it further.

To put it in a word, one would have to say that Icarus was aloof. He was friendly to a degree, in his own way, though to some, doubtless, he seemed cold and overbearing. He was highly intelligent, and what interested him he learned quickly; what did not interest him he simply ignored. As he grew older and his body grew strong, he could also work very hard — when he chose to. As soon as the People thought him old enough, he began preparing to participate in their performances. He was certainly the object of their love and affection; how much he was affected by it is a question that I cannot answer.

Several times I have mentioned the performances of the People. The People were a part of the circus and it is the business of the circus to entertain the public. They knew their business and they did it well, which was certainly one of the reasons why their position within our troupe was such an exceptional one. By now I should not have to explain that none of their performances were of the vulgar kind usually associated with so called 'side shows' or — it's painful to even use the term — 'freak galleries'. And although they certainly used suggestions from the other members of the company, most of their acts were of their own devising.

Thomas Three-Arms was a natural juggler. In addition to his three arms he also had three legs, The extra appendages were attached to the right side of his body, and although they were less well developed than his other limbs, they were not only fully functional, but also extremely quick, certainly quicker than yours or mine. By balancing himself on his middle leg, Thomas had five capable limbs with which to manipulate objects. Lying on his back, he had six. For several years, Thomas worked together with the Siamese twins, Guida and Carla. It is an understatement when I call their act spectacular. Though I probably saw it hundreds of times, I never tired of seeing it again, and after each performance I could never help but break into the wild applause that proclaims: "This is the only true world!"

One of the People's acts often left the audience so dumbfounded that they would doubt the evidence of their own eyes. Two giants, a man and a woman, come out to the center ring. In contrast to the other performers, their costumes are long and flowing, covering most of their arms and legs. They tower so high above the announcer that some people miss the first few moves in sheer wonderment. But these giants are skilled acrobats. Effortlessly they perform feats which normal people would consider utterly beyond the capacity of human beings. Seeing them swing their huge bodies from the bars is a marvel. No doubt some people notice that these bodies are not quite properly proportioned, behave somewhat awkwardly in motion, but that does not seem untoward for creatures between eight and nine feet high. The climax of the act comes as one giant thrusts the other from his shoulders — together they stand higher than anyone would have thought imaginable — wildly into the air. After a series of seemingly reckless leaps, swings, bounces, and aerial pirouettes aided by a trampoline, the second giant lands back on her feet next to the first, and together they bow stiffly to the crowd. Then, before the audience can begin to applaud, both giants suddenly tear off their clothing and — is it possible? — turn into six dwarves, who now line up in a row holding hands and bow again to the crowd. Then they scamper off before the public has recovered its wits. Drawn back by thunderous applause, they perform the second part of their act as six rather than as two people, if anything, keeping the spectators even more spellbound.

This is one act that many must see again, simply to assure themselves that their eyes did not deceive them the first time. And they are never disappointed.

Such was the world into which Icarus entered. It was a world in which those who in other circumstances had been considered deformed, crippled, ugly, had transformed themselves into extraordinary, almost superhuman, beings at whom ordinary humans sighed with envy just to watch. Seen now, twenty years after the fact, the People have perhaps taken on an almost mythical character in my mind; however, I still have clippings from the great newspapers of that era which confirm my opinion. Many, of course, still remember, and will not forget for as long as they live.

It had been clear from the start that Icarus was meant for the trapeze. Indeed, even if he had not had wings, his lean, muscular, perfectly balanced body would have destined him to that art. He began at seven, actually rather a late age to start in that profession. But it happened that he did not appear interested in the event until then. Ever patient, the People did not press him. Suddenly, one day, he began on his own. He did not ask advice, but seemed to listen when it was offered. Quickly, he developed into a very skillful artist.

He tried putting his wings to use almost from the beginning, but with little success. They did not seem to be designed properly for what he wanted to do with them. In fact, they were more of a hindrance. Nevertheless, he became such a superb trapeze artist that it mattered little. The People, however, seemed to believe that at some point he would actually begin to fly, or at least glide, with them, though most of the rest of us, myself included, thought that nonsense. We were wrong, of course.

By the time he was ten, Icarus was participating in the public performances, although he was certainly not yet comparable with the mature artists of the trapeze. At that time he was being touted as "The Winged Boy", a claim that the public did not believe until they saw him unfurl them briefly at the beginning of his act. (For some reason, he adamantly refused to let his name, Icarus, be used in the advertising.) On the trapeze, his wings were clearly evident, although they played no practical role in his act.

From the beginning, Icarus was very popular with the public and well-received by the critics. His performances were remarkable, even awe-inspiring, yet in spite of the obvious intensity of his movements, he somehow maintained a peculiar detachment that could not fail to strike the expert observer. It was as if he were so perfectly designed for this activity that it required no effort on his part, but was only a matter of letting his body follow its natural inclinations.

A couple of years later there was a change. Icarus was around twelve then and had recently started growing rapidly. One day the word spread that Icarus was flying. Curious people went to see, myself among them. Surely enough, the boy was finally beginning to put his wings to use. He was still rather awkward with them, but he was slowly learning to prolong his flight through the air by gliding with them for short distances. It was certainly marvelous, although not exactly spectacular. Certainly, his musculature had developed handsomely in the last couple of years, and the wings seemed more and more a fitting part of his body.

Slowly, Icarus improved his control and endurance. But before much longer, he decided that his practices would be closed to all spectators, claiming that their presence disturbed him — certainly a curious claim for so cool and consummate a performer. Two of the dwarves saw to it that this wish was carried out. We grumbled, but accepted this condition, knowing full well that Icarus only wanted to develop his powers more fully before displaying them to our lowly eyes.

One day it was announced that Icarus was ready to present the first public demonstration of his flying powers. At that time he was not quite fourteen years old. The place was Buda-Pest, a city that appreciates circuses perhaps more than any other. It was the final night of a seventeen day stand. No special announcement had been made, but somehow the rumor spread among circus-goers that a very special event was planned for that night. The hall was packed, overflowing. Even those of us in the company had only a vague idea of what Icarus was planning to do; I don't know if anyone knew except his partners and perhaps Nora. We knew that he would fly as none of us had ever seen him fly before, but of course we couldn't really imagine what that would be like. We shuffled about tensely all evening, constantly looking in to check the progress of the program. As expected, his was the last performance. The caller announced him simply: "Icarus, the Flying Man."

Icarus! The Flying Man! Never before had he let his name be proclaimed to the public. So he was now a man!

The Great Hall in Buda-Pest is certainly one of the grandest buildings in the world for a circus. The trapeze bars were arranged for Icarus that night in an unusual fashion. There were quite a number of them; they marched across the high roof of the building from one corner to the other; the ones at the far end were set much closer to the ground than the others, perhaps only half way up from the arena floor. They were not spaced exceptionally far apart, however, and I didn't see that any unusual amount of flying would be called for.

Suddenly the artist appeared, swinging gracefully from one trapeze to the next, traversing the upper level of the hall from one end to the other. But it was not Icarus, it was Sonja, the young woman with whom he had lately been training. Then Icarus appeared too, and a few of the crowd started applauding; the rest were spellbound: certainly his movements were the most masterful that any of us had ever seen. Sonja was scarcely less perfect. Together they performed an unbelievable duet high above our heads, a symphony, almost, in the intricacy, grace and power of its movements. Back and forth they sailed underneath the rooftop, crossing the entire hall several times from end to end. I began to notice how Icarus was indeed using his wings, not exactly flying, but skillfully maneuvering himself out of the plane of the trapeze and back, weaving intricate patterns around

Sonja. To myself I said: "Well, my son, you have learned to use your gift."

Then a terrible thing happened.

Sonja had crossed the hall to where the low bars hung, which had hitherto been ignored. There she cavorted alone for a few moments, while Icarus displayed his virtuosity some distance away. Suddenly she swung herself up and back towards the higher bars, trying to regain the upper level. It was a superb move, beautifully executed, but from the start clearly not strong enough. She would not be able to reach any of the higher bars, she would not even come close. I jumped to my feet aghast, my heart rushing to my mouth. A cry went up from the crowd as Sonja reached the peak of her climb and began falling — over a hundred feet to the floor. Icarus, at the other end of the hall, was helpless to save her.

Then, suddenly, he was flying — flying! — on his great, beautiful wings, now stretched out for the first time fully. In one startling motion he sped across the great hall, sweeping down low to reach Sonja. And caught her! Perfectly, superbly. Then, with Sonja holding him about the waist and by the legs, he gave two powerful beats with his wings and sailed back up to the top of the hall. There she released herself from him, spinning away, then straightening out to grasp one of the trapezes. Icarus alighted at one of the neighboring bars, and there they swung for a while, serenely, as if nothing had happened.

It was, of course, a well-rehearsed and perfectly executed act. Many people continued to believe it a near accident until the pair had repeated the same scene several times, in different variations. It was later reported that a number of people in the audience fainted that night.

The rest of the performance I need not describe. Along with even greater ones, it has been recorded on film and shown around the world; nearly everyone has now seen these films at one time or another. Nevertheless, it is difficult to conceive of the effect that that original performance had on those who saw it in Buda-Pest.

After Icarus and Sonja had finished, it took the crowd about half a minute to recover enough even to applaud. Which they then continued to do steadily for almost five minutes. And another ten or fifteen minutes went by before they all managed to leave the hall. No doubt they hoped that the artists would return for an encore — which they gladly would have done, had they not been utterly exhausted.

Most of the events of the following years are now common knowledge, or at least well documented, and I need not dwell on them. Suffice it to say that Icarus' act quickly became our chief attraction, indeed, the greatest attraction of any circus in the world; and that our company was soon known simply as 'the circus of the flying man'. Within a few years, Icarus was able to glide half a mile, starting from a height of just a few hundred feet, and had furthermore acquired considerable maneuvering ability. His skill on the trapeze had long surpassed that of any other person, living or dead. There never had been a one like him, and it was certain that there never would be another.

All this time he continued to perform with Sonja, who, it must be noted, was also regarded as one of the greatest trapeze artists of all time. In fact, amongst the knowledgeable, she was often considered Icarus' superior. There is much more that I ought to say about Sonja, but I know this is not the place ... Before many more years at all had passed, the press began reporting rumors of a love affair between the two. There was certainly truth in this; however, the 'facts' they reported were invariably false. Perhaps the only person who knew much of this was Magnus, who before his death told me a little. I shall endeavor to relate some of it later.

It is generally supposed that with his fame and success assured, Icarus became very much of a prima donna, the prototypical self-centered, willful, volatile artist. I must protest this judgment. It reflects a total misunderstanding of the person I knew, perhaps a basic misconception of art and artists in general. In truth, I cannot say that the man of seventeen was really much different from the boy of seven. True, he was older, more experienced, his body more developed and better coordinated; he had attained a certain niche in a certain world. The basic underlying character was the same, however. If he was aloof, it was because he was born an alien and seemed fated to remain so for his earthly life. At the height of his fame he was no more and no less proud than he had been when he first came to us; it just happened that he had attained a status where his pride was finally paid its due — which was really nothing other than the basic respect that should underlie the relations between any human beings. Certainly he maintained a rather detached attitude towards his principal physical activity just as a fish might be regarded as having a detached view of the act of swimming. I can testify that he was aware and considerate of his fellow men (if I may use that term) to a degree that you and I would do well to attain more frequently. I don't mean to defend Icarus by any means, I simply must take this opportunity to refute some of the nonsense spread by thoughtless people and by the press. On the whole, I think his life and deeds can speak for themselves, only let the misconceptions be exposed as such.

About five years after Icarus' triumphant performance at Buda-Pest — that is, when he was around nineteen — he and Sonja separated themselves from our circus company. It is commonly believed that he now considered himself 'too good' to work with a mere circus, that he wanted to be the star of his own show, to make more money, etc. I will simply state the facts without comments. At the time that he left, Icarus had been 'too good' for us for many years, certainly since Buda-Pest, perhaps even from the very beginning. He knew it, the People knew it, everyone in the company knew it. 'Too good' is not the right term. We and he were doing entirely different things. We were a group of people who with much work had developed highly unusual skills, and we travelled about, displaying them to the world. He was simply a being — I deliberately avoid the word human — who had been set amongst us and who looked roughly similar. What we perceived as his unprecedented ability was simply the consequence of his natural unfolding, his reaching towards whatever fulfillment was to be his to hold. The trapeze, the circus, were simply incidental experiences, perhaps even hindrances to his proper development. As for being a star, that too was an irrelevance. After two years on their own, he and Sonja stopped giving public performances. Note that they did not stop performing, they merely stopped doing it in front of audiences. As for money, it alternately puzzled or amused him, depending on his mood. In the early days, he had simply given his earnings to Magnus or Nora and let them buy what they thought he needed out of it; whatever was left over went to the People. Later his income was paid directly into a fund which Magnus administered, and Icarus was aware neither of the amounts involved nor of what became of it.

So much for such nonsense. Now let me return to the thread of my story. As I mentioned, around the time that Icarus was nineteen, he and Sonja decided to leave the company. A sad, a difficult decision: although he was not really part of mankind, we were the only home, the only family he had ever known. He basically felt that he did not belong in a circus anymore, if he had indeed ever belonged. Of course, he would continue his work; it merely seemed inappropriate to be doing it in the context of a circus. It was a tearful leave-taking; I think even Icarus shared in the tears for once. Of course it was the People who most hated to see him go. He was, after all, their foremost son. He took about a dozen of them with him to manage the mundane affairs of the new company.

Then they quit. At first it was merely a vacation. Then the vacation was prolonged, and finally it was announced that they had retired. The world, needless to say, was dumbfounded. To us it was no surprise. Through the People accompanying Icarus we learned that he and Sonja were still flying, but that they were not doing it in front of outsiders anymore.

Then they flew away. Or, at least, that is what the stories claim. I was skeptical myself until I heard through Magnus that it was indeed true. In fact, their departure was actually much like most of the reports describe it, although I still doubt that many of the details presented in the popular accounts are literally true. Away they flew. Into the blue. Sonja, of course, couldn't really fly, but evidently Icarus could do well enough for both of them. How long he had been able to do that is something that I often wonder about. Where did they go? Mostly to places where people are few. They visited all of the continents and were occasionally sighted; there are even a couple of photographs of them that appear to be authentic. On the other hand, many of the reported sightings were no doubt purely imaginary. There may be some truth in the reports that some deranged person actually fired shots at them, although it is not clear what the consequences were for the shooter. Icarus and Sonja at any rate, were not harmed. As we know, this went on for upwards of six months, although in my opinion, all of the details given in the press should be regarded as completely fictitious.

And then Sonja returned alone. It was claimed that she was pregnant — which she was. But what had happened? Had the lovers quarreled? Had Sonja decided that she was not meant to fly? Had the inhuman experience driven her to madness? She didn't tell; no one knows. Icarus was soon back too, looking for her. She acted as if she didn't want to be found. Three weeks later, she was dead, the unborn child dead. People wondered what the child would have been like. It is claimed with some authority that it would have had wings.

Icarus vanished again. Some thought he had killed her. Actually, her death could have been murder, accident, or suicide: she fell from a height.

You would think by now that this story would be about over, that very soon I must report Icarus' death and then wrap the whole thing up. I wish I could, but as you know, Icarus still had another fifteen years to live. He remained out of sight for a year or two. Actually he was in contact with the People and with Nora during most of this period, he just didn't make his whereabouts known. There are some strong indications that he was living right in our midst all that time, although with his obvious physical differences this is a bit hard to believe. Anyway, he finally returned. It was a rather quiet return. In some way his story had lost much of its glamor with Sonja's death. I spoke to him on a number of occasions, but he always seemed rather distant. He was quite adept at not answering my questions without offending me excessively. I don't think that he even confided much to the People, but then he never had.

Shortly afterwards, he began taking up with scientists. For years they had been begging to study him, but he had steadfastly refused. Now, suddenly, he put himself into their hands, submitted wholeheartedly to their investigations. And they studied him for years. And wrote a lot of books

about him. Etcetera. Etcetera. I find this a very uninteresting part of his life, but supposedly they can now tell us exactly why he was the way he was. I often wonder why he let
himself be subjected to all of this malarkey. The only explanation I can offer is that he hoped that they would provide
him with some vital information. Vital for what purposes, I
can only speculate. During these years he reportedly
refrained from flying except for their experiments. Knowing
what I know of him, that is very hard to believe, yet I am now
pretty certain that it is true.

And now he is dead. In years he could not have been
much more than thirty-five. No one knows whether his
death was accident or suicide. After years without strenu-
ous, long-distance flying, it certainly did not seem very wise
of him to start again by flying off over the sea. I must say
that it looks very much like a deliberate death, but then I
can't rule out the possibility of an error in judgment, or the
failure of his powers. If I recall correctly, this is the same way
that the original Icarus died.

And so that should be the end of this story. However, I
still have a few further scraps of information to relate,
though with some misgivings. Most of this material is due to
Magnus. He had perhaps been closer to Sonja and Icarus
than anyone else, and shared their secrets if anyone did. An
aged and childless dwarf, I think he regarded them as his
children, as the noblest issue of his life. The news of Sonja's
death and Icarus' subsequent disappearance left him a broken man and hastened the already impending end. I think
these tragic events affected his mind, so it is difficult for me
to separate fact from mere speculation in his revelations.
Nevertheless, I set them down, with the minimum of personal interpretation, and hope that they will serve to shed
some light on the lives of these two unusual beings.

Sonja's parents had come from a small country on the

Baltic Sea that once had borne some name like Livonia or Kuronia. I don't know what it's called today. Her family had all been circus people, mostly acrobats and trapeze artists, perhaps for generations, and it was assumed that she would follow suit. Which was easy enough for her to do as she had a natural gift for the art. She was, in fact, a prodigy herself, perhaps (in consideration of her inherent physical limitations) even more so than Icarus. Then, when she was about seven or eight, there was a terrible tragedy in the family: her uncle and four of her cousins fell while executing their celebrated highwire balancing act. The uncle and two cousins died; the survivors were disabled for life. Sonja and her parents were witnesses to this terrible event. It was years before any of them ventured up again.

I recall when her family joined our company, when Icarus was ten or eleven, but I didn't really take particular note of her until she became his favorite partner. Sonja and Icarus took to each other from the start. In her he saw, finally, one of his own kind, his sister-brother, one who was also made to fly. Of course, she lacked his own peculiar gift, but that was of little relevance. Having spent most of his life among the People, he saw that as a mere accident of fate, certainly not as a deformity. She had the essence of wings, but merely lacked their physical manifestation. He became convinced that in time she would actually learn to fly without physical wings, and in the meantime he would make up for their lack himself. Sonja, apparently, came to believe this also, though perhaps with less conviction than Icarus. Being the one who had less, she found it hard to accept from him. Having an absolutely unshakeable belief in the underlying correctness of the universe, he found it difficult — perhaps impossible — to comprehend that she did not always share this conviction with him.

Their love for each other — if I can call it that — is probably not comprehensible in human terms. Furthermore, we must consider that they were the only two creatures of their species on the earth. So I will pass over it without further words that add or explain nothing.

It's possible that they looked upon their years as performers as mere training which would have been difficult or impossible to obtain any other way. Or maybe they were just so caught up in the immediacy of the experience of the trapeze that they did not even stop to think any other thing.

When they finally flew off together, it was the inevitable break with the world of others, of us unwinged, merely human beings. And there was no need to come back ever again. However, Sonja doubted herself. She saw herself as incomplete, unworthy. Her physical deformity was too much to overcome. Apparently, with Icarus' assistance and encouragement, she made some sort of efforts to fly by herself, but I cannot even imagine what this could have been like. Did she somehow believe that she might fly using only pure will? Icarus never doubted that Sonja would come to fly some day, and he found it difficult to comprehend her self-doubts. Rejecting herself, feeling her efforts were hopeless, Sonja fled. Failing to see the basis for her action, Icarus followed. For two months, she avoided him, then, finding herself pregnant with his winged child, she jumped off of a cliff: it was a desperate attempt to fly by herself; it was the only way she could come to be his equal.

Of course, she was defying certain immutable laws and perished. Afterwards, Icarus spent fifteen years trying to find something out; we don't know what — perhaps something we can't even understand, perhaps something foolish, perhaps nothing at all. One wonders, when he threw himself into the air for the final time, was it the ultimate affirmation of his life, or had he, too, finally been defeated?

She Sleeps, I Dream

The baby's name was to have been Hadley Samuels McPherson if a boy, Nora Wright McPherson if a girl. When he asked the doctor whether it was a boy or a girl, there was an almost imperceptible pause before Dr. Davies replied, "Girl", during which Roger McPherson knew that something was wrong. Yet before that perception had time to reach his conscious mind, words had already flown through his head, words of rejoicing, spoken to an unseen person in response to an unheard question: "Her name is Nora!"

They took their misfortune well, considering the circumstances, considering the fact that they were a young couple very much in love, considering that this was their first child, and also, due to complications in the delivery, necessarily her last. He was a brilliant young anthropologist, just beginning his career at Harvard University, she a poet, a painter, a beautiful woman who to many sometimes still seemed a precocious child. The pregnancy and the labor had been difficult, but she, and he, had borne it courageously, with humor. They certainly deserved better, thought Patrick Davies, than this creature whom they called Nora.

Her case was not unprecedented, but certainly very rare, and in the literature of teratology, almost undocumented. Despite his heartfelt sympathy for the family, Dr. Davies also experienced a certain professional thrill at the opportunity afforded for scientific investigation; but this he succeeded in concealing from the family. The unusual circumstance in this case was that Nora seemed strong, healthy. Both heads cried vigorously, demanded nourishment. It was a case of identical twins who had incompletely separated, whose differentiation had extended only to the head and then stopped. From previous experience, a life expectancy of only hours or days was to be predicted. But this one looked like an exception. Barring complications — which should be regarded as the rule in such cases, stressed Dr. Davies — Nora might survive for years.

But is it one creature or two? thought Elizabeth Wright McPherson as she offered her breasts, both of them at once, to Nora's demanding mouths. True, in the first instant of the first feeding, a slight shiver of revulsion had gone through her thin yet strong body. But she understood its origins, set it aside in the next moment utterly mastered, and offered her milk and her love to her daughter or daughters. For three years, she and Roger McPherson had travelled to distant parts of the world and lived with peoples whose ways of life, to Elizabeth Wright's fellow Bostonians, would surely have seemed grotesque, monstrous even. Yet towards many of them Elizabeth had come to feel, later or sooner, more sympathy, closer bonds than to most of the graduates of elite universities who were now her daily associates. While her husband had discoursed on their ways in his books, she had celebrated their culture, their religion, their songs, dances, masks, costumes in her poems and paintings. And many more people now knew, for example, of the Tsingli people of the Upper Volta Plateau through her book of poems *The Sand Gods* than through Roger McPherson's scholarly treatises. How would Nora have been accepted by the Tsingli, wondered Elizabeth, as she nursed her child? Probably as a divine gift, a token of special favor to her people from the moon spirit, to be cherished for the present, in time to be regarded as a shaman whose opinion would be consulted before any major undertaking. Should Elizabeth's love, her reverence for her own infant child be any less? The only thing she might be ashamed of was the vestiges of her bourgeois upbringing that could even have caused her to think otherwise.

Roger McPherson's acceptance of Nora was initially less than complete. He had, consciously or unconsciously, wanted an heir, intellectual and spiritual more than material, and his initial reaction to the child was tinged with anger and resentment. Furthermore, Elizabeth could never bear another child; indeed, this single abnormal pregnancy may have affected her health permanently. He could accept Nora as a human creature, but he found it difficult to accept the fact that Nora was his daughter. Why him? What had he done to deserve this?

It was Elizabeth who finally showed him his mistake, though it took months, and in the end it was his love and devotion to her which finally transferred itself to the child. But once having made the emotional decision to accept Nora as his daughter, to offer her his love, he no longer held back, but loved her as wholeheartedly as did his wife. So the vision of the poet prevailed where the erudition of the scholar faltered.

And Nora? She grew, she prospered. Had she any reason to pursue the struggle for existence any less vigorously than any other woman's child? But a strange thing happened after just three, four weeks. The baby's second head, the one on their left, Nora's right, went to sleep, never to wake up again. It was still alive, but seemed in a state of permanent somnolence, an expression of infantile bliss maintaining itself without change. Until then, both heads had played virtually equal roles, both expressing lively personalities, or perhaps the same personality twofold. Now, suddenly, from

one day to the next, Nora's right head had withdrawn from
the physical world, had elected to spend the remainder of its
life in a state of contemplation or unconsciousness.

Elizabeth was troubled by the unexpected occurrence.
Gently, she tied to rouse the sleeping head. But her efforts,
her slaps, only annoyed the other head and set it crying, and
so she desisted. But Dr. Davies was consulted, and he examined, tested, hypothesized. Finally, he told the McPhersons
what they already knew by then, that the right head might
never awaken again, even though it might continue to live in
a vegetative fashion; and that it had stopped growing and
would probably never reach physical maturity. He also mentioned the possibility of surgery to remove the dormant head
— a risky business, surely, but the only way that Nora, if she
survived, would ever lead a normal life. He, at any rate, was
willing to give it a try; if the baby did not survive, well, perhaps that might in some ways be less tragic than if she were
allowed to continue life as she was.

But the McPhersons would not hear of it. Dr. Davies
could not convince them that the benefits outweighed the
risks, and after a while he stopped trying. He consoled himself instead with publishing, with her parents' permission,
two papers on Nora's case; and with discussing with his colleagues how well the McPhersons had adapted to their peculiar misfortune.

Some years went by. Nora continued to grow, remained
healthy and strong; the sleeping head did not awaken, nor
did it grow any larger. Eventually, when Nora was grown,
the dormant head, still infantile in size and appearance,
would be only an appendage, not excessively prominent, on
the right side of her neck. In certain attire it might be hidden
altogether; on other occasions people might even, on first
glance, mistake Nora for a mother carrying her sleeping baby
in an unorthodox but not impossible fashion. But few of

them, if once they had the chance to look more closely, would be able to suppress a gasp, or even, all too often, a scream of fear.

Why is it that we fear the monstrous, even when it does not in any way threaten us? Is it perhaps that after a certain age we close ourselves off to true novelty? Or is it rather an unwelcome reminder that the universe, which we would like to think of as orderly and benign, is revealed as being essentially capricious and unpredictable; and that we perhaps exist and prosper, not at its sufferance even, but almost as though by accident, and perhaps for ends, which, if we knew them, might seem alien and terrible to us?

So Nora grew. She remained healthy, but Elizabeth never fully recovered her own health. Once he had accepted her, Roger was proud of Nora and planned a bright future for her. There was certainly no indication that she would be physically or mentally retarded in any way. After all, she did carry half of his genes and half of Elizabeth's. There was no reason why, if given a chance, she could not surpass their own many and varied accomplishments. In fact, if Roger had been allowed to have his way unchecked, he might have made her into one of those prodigies who can recite Latin and Greek epics by the time they are seven. But again, Elizabeth prevailed, channeled and balanced her husband's energy and good intentions, and convinced him that genius, if that was what he saw in his daughter, was really no blessing unless it was part of a whole and happy human being.

But Elizabeth did not have many more years to live. In spite of the strength and resolve of her spirit, her body was frail, was mortal. Following Nora's birth she was plagued by a series of illnesses and physical ailments; they were never anything unusual or serious, but always seemed to linger for longer than they should have, to lead to complications which in an ordinarily healthy person would never had occurred.

Although this certainly depressed her spirits and inhibited her work, she became accustomed to it too, accepted it, and learned to live within her physical limitations, tried to respond to her body's weakness with humor and detachment.

When Nora was not quite five years old, Elizabeth contracted pneumonia and died within a month. She seemed strong and happy until the very last, but there is evidence that she knew all the while that the end was coming, and she went to lengths to conceal her suffering and impending death from Roger. One may surmise this, at any rate, from her very last works, that extraordinary collection of poems entitled *What the Wind Whispers*, which she wrote during her final three weeks and left for Roger to discover after her death. In it she tried to distill the wisdom of her short but varied stay on earth into a message of love for Roger and Nora, of thankfulness for having lived, of hope for the future — for Roger, for Nora, for the world.

These poems were never published until many years later, long after Roger's death, by Nora herself. But during the weeks and months that followed, they were perhaps what sustained Roger in his grief more than anything else, what saved him from despair and from the suicide which he later admitted he had contemplated following Elizabeth's death. For how could he kill himself when with her last words she had told him that his own life, fully and consciously lived in each of its moments, would be the finest expression that he could make of his love for her? To deny himself life would thus have been to deny her and his love for her. Not that grief is to be shunned: No! Death is our sharpest and dearest reminder of the preciousness, the never-again-to-be-repeated, never-again-to-be-enjoyed miracle of temporal existence. To deny grief is to deny the essence of that miracle, yet to surrender to that grief, to allow it to drive one to his own death, does no honor to living or dead. For if grief is partly sorrow at not having loved enough while the chance was given, what we can learn from it is not to allow that to happen ever again, beginning with the present moment. In that way we can truly honor the dead: by intensifying our own lives, which is the only way in which they continue to live. So spoke Elizabeth Wright to Roger McPherson, and later, to others of us, in *What the Wind Whispers*.

Nora, too, was deeply stricken by Elizabeth's death, though in a seemingly less desperate way than Roger. For her mother had clearly told her to expect it, and she saw its necessity within the scheme of things. This did not mitigate the tears at all, but rather lent them some understanding, and finally, peace and inspiration. For Nora saw much clearer than Roger that the best way she could honor her mother was through her own life. Nor did she doubt her ability to do so adequately: for in her last months, more than anything else, Elizabeth had sought to instill in her daughter a sense of self-esteem which later proved to be unshakeable.

So Elizabeth was buried, Roger got past the loss, Nora grew older. Soon it was time for her to go to school. She had, of course, already received a considerable amount of schooling at home; she was, in fact, well beyond the scholastic achievements of her age-mates before she even began, but Roger, convinced that contact with other children of her age was absolutely necessary for her development, sent her off to the public schools.

That lasted just three weeks.

He had found what he judged to be a relatively enlightened school, spoken in advance to all of Nora's teachers about her abnormality, and brought her to school on the first day with trepidation, certainly, but also with determination. Nora herself was utterly excited. The excitement did not last out the week. After the first day Nora said: "I don't think the other children like us very much. They make fun of my baby sister." (Nora often spoke of herself in the plural, and always referred to the sleeping head as her sister.) By the end of the first week, she had several incidents to report in which the other children had harassed her verbally. Strangely, to Roger, she did not seem very upset about this, or even surprised. Elizabeth had done her work well: Nora well knew that she was different from the other children because she always carried her 'sister' with her, and that she must expect others to stare, to ask questions, to poke fun.

By the end of the second week, the principal of the school had telephoned Roger and wondered whether it might not be better to send Nora to a special school where her handicap would be better accepted. With the best intentions in the world, he said, it was not going to be possible to get all of the other children to accept Nora; in fact, he thought, her continued attendance was starting to upset some of the more sensitive children; and some of the other parents were getting worried, if not actually complaining. Roger spoke to Nora, asked her if she would like to stay home or to go to another school. But Nora saw no need to make such a change, seemed to be content with her present school. The hostility of the other children did not seem to disturb her greatly.

In the middle of the third week, Nora quit school entirely. She did not want to go back, would probably have refused to return. She had been attacked after school by a group of children, who had thrown stones at her. Her hands, her face were bruised and bloody. But what upset her the most, it seemed, was that all the while she felt that they had been attacking her sister, who was defenseless, unable to protect herself. And Nora, apparently, did not even attempt to protect the rest of her body: her only thought was to shield her sleeping sister from the flying rocks. And the teacher who rescued her had a strange report to make: he claimed that as he carried the hurt but uncomplaining Nora back to the school building, he claimed that the sleeping face was wet with tears, that he had actually seen it crying ...

If that was so, it was the first time in six years that the dormant head had shown any sign of active life. Roger doubted the report, but secretly he worried that the sleeping head might indeed awaken some day, just as suddenly as it had gone to sleep, and he wondered how that would further complicate his daughter's already complicated existence. Perhaps it would have been better after all if Dr. Davies had been allowed to operate when she was younger. Perhaps it was still not too late.

Roger investigated several special schools where Nora might be better accepted. But in the end he elected to continue her education at home; it was, after all, clearly no defect of mind or body that hindered her learning. So for the next several years Nora was taught by a series of special tutors, all of them carefully selected by Roger, many of them outstanding educators or scholars. And he arranged for her to have some contact with other children, often different sorts of handicapped children, and he furthermore took considerable time from his own busy schedule to work and play with her.

So in her first ten years, it should be noted, Nora had a very rich, in many respects an ideal, home environment in which to grow and to learn. Roger McPherson spared no expense in order to make it so. And by then he was, in spite of himself, a fairly wealthy man — he who ostensibly cared so little for material goods or pleasures — through the success of both his and his wife's books. The only things that were notably lacking to Nora were a mother, and very much contact with other children.

But the following twelve years of her life Nora remembered as something like a nightmare. Roger died when she was ten. Unlike his wife, his death was nearly a year in consummating itself, and was most painful and troubling both for himself and for those around him.

Roger had contracted a rare viral disease during one of his stays in Africa. It had first manifested itself some years before, but in a mild form, no worse than a typical flu, and affecting him noticeably for only a few weeks. He quickly responded to drugs and soon recovered. But several years later there was a relapse. Again, the treatments were seemingly successful, but the disease was now diagnosed as chronic and the drugs merely held it in abatement. But the virus soon affected his nervous system, and even though its onslaught could be slowed and controlled, its effect was now permanent, and at some point would begin to make itself evident in Roger's physical functioning.

The process of deterioration lasted a full year. Roger's speech was among the first faculties to be noticeably affected, then certain motor activities were impaired and he could no longer move about without assistance. Finally, he began to lose verbal and language ability altogether as the disease started to affect his brain. During the last month his existence was mostly vegetative. He saw the end coming upon him many months before and would gladly have hastened it, but by then he was too weak and no longer physically able to kill himself; and those around him who could have helped him, refused to honor his pleas for mercy.

Nora saw all of this. Nurses and helpers were hired to tend to Roger, and they tried to keep her away, tried to keep her from witnessing the tragedy. Uselessly: not only was she easily able to outwit them whenever she wanted, but Roger insisted on seeing her often. Once he realized that his remaining time on earth was limited, he wanted to insure that Nora was prepared to continue her life without his protection.

She had been prepared for years. In his more lucid moments, Roger realized this, and he spoke to her frankly of what was happening to him, what would happen to her after he died. He spoke to her, at times, as he once had spoken to Elizabeth, whom Nora was coming to resemble more and more with each passing day.

Unfortunately, Roger's judgment was also affected by his illness, or else he miscalculated completely in his choice for Nora's guardian: He chose one of Elizabeth's uncles, Elias Whitmore, a prominent psychologist who lived in California, whom he knew by academic reputation, though hardly as a human being. This man had never even met Nora, nor did he ever do so; his only two acts in Nora's regard were to consign her to the care of a state institution, and to place Roger's wealth, willed entirely to Nora, into a trust fund administered by his personal attorney.

(ii)

So for the next twelve years Nora McPherson was imprisoned in the Eastern State School for the Severely Handicapped and Mentally Defective. The word 'imprisoned' was her own; the institution she would later refer to as the 'concentration camp'.

She never spoke much of her experiences at that place, and when she did, it was with a sort of barely suppressed anger. Her only positive comment on those years was that they taught her how to pretend and how to sew. But we can easily surmise what her life must have been like for those twelve years. Her compatriots were people who were either almost totally disabled physically — unable to move about on their own, unable to feed or dress themselves — or who were unable to communicate normally because of various impediments of speech or hearing. Nonetheless, Nora claimed that she succeeded in communicating perfectly well with a good number of inmates who were considered by their tenders to be utterly and hopelessly non-verbal. How she did this may become evident later from some of the hints she dropped concerning her 'sister'.

During most of her stay, or imprisonment, at the Eastern State School, Nora was confined to a six by twelve foot cell which for the first seven years she shared with another woman, twenty years her senior, who had lost all ability to use her limbs and whose sight and hearing were furthermore severely impaired. Nora's cell, unlike many of the others, had the luxury of its own washing and toilet facilities. When she 'misbehaved' however, which happened often in the first several years, less frequently thereafter, she was punished by being confined to a tiny, dark, unheated, windowless chamber with padded floor and walls — the 'hole' — which did not even have sufficient room for a grown person to stretch out in fully. If she was unable to control her bowel movements while in the hole — her stays lasted from six or eight hours to several days — she would simply have to wallow in her own excrement, only to be berated for her filthiness when she was finally released and then forced to clean up after herself.

Drugs were another major part of life at the 'school'. At first she took them willingly, curiously even, wondering what this strange ritual was all about that everyone participated in. But as soon as she realized what effect they were having on her, she refused, angrily and brazenly, hurling the pills at the attendant and stomping away.

That was, of course, useless. Not only did they administer the drugs forcefully, but in punishment for her rebellion she was sent to the hole for the first time. But she would not give in: again she hurled the pills to the ground, spit out the liquids that they had forced into her mouth. It took both the other patients prevailing upon her, as well as her own realizations, to convince her that this form of resistance was useless. So she soon learned how to obediently accept and apparently swallow the medicine, then to dispose of it secretly as soon as the attention of the attendants was diverted elsewhere. And she became very proficient at simulating the different effects of the various drugs, so that there was never any suspicion aroused that she was not receiving her medicine as prescribed. So complete was her subterfuge that by the time she left the institution, she was considered a model patient, one who was allowed unusual freedom in moving about the buildings and who was appreciated and praised for her assistance with the other inmates.

But for the first several years, until she was fifteen or sixteen, there were frequent relapses, frequent breakdowns in the co-operative facade that she created for herself. For example, she ran away twice. One time she was gone for two weeks. She managed somehow to get as far as Providence, 150 miles away, where she begged on the streets and lived out of trash cans before allowing herself to be rescued by a kindly stranger, who, of course, promptly betrayed her. Carrying her sister with her as she did, there was no way that she could avoid attention and scrutiny.

But eventually, she adapted completely, it seemed, to the ways of the 'school', followed the path of least resistance. This was to discover what those in charge of her wanted and to give it to them with as little opposition as possible, hoping that in return they would leave her in peace. The only break-down in this strategy was when it came to a conflict between the demands of the attendants and her loyalty to the other inmates. For she could never make herself turn against one of her comrades. To get out of such situations she would sometimes feign a disability or lack of understanding that would hopefully cause her to be relieved from an onerous duty.

When Nora was seventeen, her cellmate, Cynthia Wexler, died. Nora took care of her almost to the end. Indeed, part of Nora's eventual good relations with the staff of the 'school' was due to the fact that she often took upon herself the bur-den of caring for some of the more troublesome inmates. Even when Nora first came, Cynthia could not move around at all; if she wanted to go outside, which most inmates were permitted to do only twice a week for half an hour at a time, she would have to be rolled out in a kind of reclining wheel-chair, a rolling bed on wheels. Nora took charge of this, as well as of washing Cynthia, helping her eat and relieve her-self. Cynthia's vision and hearing were not good, and wors-ening, but in the first years she still had full command of speech. Eventually, Cynthia was no longer able to hear Nora's voice at all, nor even to read her lips, and the two communicated by means of touch, making signs in each other's hands, or by reading lips with their fingers. Perhaps also by other means as well.

It was a great sorrow for Nora that they took Cynthia away just before she died, that she had to die alone. Nora protested vigorously, even tried to interfere, disregarding Cynthia's admonitions that it was alright to let her go. And she would probably have been punished for her misbehavior, but for once her privileged position brought her leniency: after all, it was her companion of seven years who had died, mightn't they excuse her for once for breaking the rules?

For the next five years Nora did not share her cell with anyone, though she spent much of her time ministering to and helping the other inmates. Another thing that happened was that she rediscovered books and began reading again, for the first time since she was ten. The institution had a library which ostensibly was partly for the use and edification of the patients, but in fact was practically inaccessible to them. When Nora first heard of it, she asked to be allowed to go there, only to be told that it was located in a part of the building which she wasn't allowed to enter. However, one attendant said that if Nora would tell her what book she wanted, she would try to find it and bring it to her. Nora didn't know what books there were, so she asked for any book of poetry, especially one by a poet named Elizabeth Wright. The attendant said she would see, but after two weeks she still had done nothing, and then she was transferred to another part of the 'school', and Nora never saw her again. So Nora repeated her request to another attendant, a young man; he never brought her any books either, though he did talk her into attending a bible study class three nights a week, which Nora quit, disgusted, after two weeks, immediately sensing the contradiction between the behavior being preached there and that practiced towards the inmates of the 'school'.

So other than some glossy picture magazines that circulated amongst the inmates, Nora was unable to get her hands on any printed matter for a number of years. The only real educational opportunity at the school were classes in certain manual skills and crafts, of which Nora was most interested in sewing. She was never permitted to have her own needles or other sewing materials, but she could work in the crafts room, watched over by an attendant but otherwise undisturbed, for hours at a time. Most of the other patients spent their time watching television, which was readily available to them, almost ubiquitous even, at almost any hour of day or night. But Nora generally disliked television, although there were times when she seemed to watch it spellbound.

Then, after Cynthia's death, the energy which she had devoted to her cellmate became more diffuse and was expended more and more in helping the staff care for some of the more difficult patients. Nora showed no hesitation in performing chores which the staff disdained, such as cleaning up excrement, and so she won their appreciation and eventually favor. When she was finally accorded the coveted privilege of entering that part of the building that housed the library, and finally the library itself, her joy was unbounded, or bounded only by the fear that this privilege might suddenly and capriciously by withdrawn from her, whether she remained helpful and cooperative or not.

But for once her luck held, or perhaps she had completely understood and adapted to the ways of the institution. She was allowed to visit the library any time it was open and was even allowed to take the books to her cell. Delicious privilege! She was gladly willing to spend long hours wiping up vomit, scrubbing toilets, helping to exercise inmates in return for the privilege of being able, in the late hours of the night or early in the morning, to read a book of her choosing in the quiet of her cell.

She read voraciously, but without tutelage or direction. Her favorites were fiction and poetry, but she read much non-fiction also. She was able, in the course of four years, to teach herself a smattering of many subjects, including geology, Spanish, Latin, chemistry, electricity, history, archaeology, algebra and math, and more. But oftentimes, she would unknowingly pick a book that was quite beyond her level and try, with uncertain success, to make some sense of it. She read, for example, half a dozen high school chemistry texts before she was able, by inference, to learn enough math to make the quantitative parts intelligible. Only much later did she discover the algebra book that would have provided the key. In vain she sought some information about her own body and the troubling changes she was observing in it, but the information she sought was apparently omitted from the introductory texts — deliberately, it seemed to her; in the more advanced books it was stated in such terms that could only frustrate someone without a college education or medical training. Yet still she managed to understand much.

Nora's release from the Eastern State School for the Severely Handicapped and Mentally Defective came suddenly, unexpectedly, completely without warning. From one day to the next she was free. She was then twenty-two years old.

One day — she was mopping the floor in one of the eating areas — a nurse walked up to her and said: "You have a visitor."

A visitor? Nora had never had a visitor before. Who would visit her? Who did she even know on the outside? It could only be Elias Whitmore, whom she had never seen but rightly blamed for her imprisonment, instinctively loathed. She gritted her teeth, tried to control her trembling, and followed the nurse.

It was not Elias Whitmore, it was his son, Farley Whitmore. Elias Whitmore had died over a month before. His principal heir, Farley, who was twenty-six years old at the time, had been an unsuccessful medical student, and was now a jazz musician and something of a vagabond and bohemian, to the end a disappointment to his father. He had decided to inform himself about this strange young woman, reportedly feeble-minded or crazy, that his father had been guardian to but whom no one had ever seen, his own cousin, the daughter of his illustrious relative Elizabeth Wright.

He explained to Nora — once he had determined that she was capable of carrying on an intelligent conversation — he explained that her status was currently in a legal limbo. He, Farley, could if he chose, take over the responsibilities of being her guardian, though he felt little inclination to do so at present. Or he could let her revert to being a ward of the state, in which case some responsible professional would be assigned the duty of representing her wishes to the school or other agencies. The whole situation was unfamiliar and exceedingly uncomfortable to him, he explained, but he felt that he at least had the responsibility of meeting Nora and seeing what feelings, if any, she had in this regard. (So as not to complicate the situation further, he purposely failed to mention Nora's trust fund, which even after the attorney's sizable administration fee, had grown to a substantial fortune.)

What did Nora want to do? She glanced around to make sure that there were no staff people were around to hear her, and fighting back her tears, she exclaimed:

"I want to leave here! Please help me get out of here! Why, why am I being kept in this prison?"

Farley could not answer her question. In fact, he ended up speaking to her for several hours, and was most impressed, even charmed, by her, and through all of it he could not come up with a single reason why Nora was there. In the end, he promised to help her, agreed to become her guardian at least long enough for her to be released and to recover her legal rights. He was, indeed, deeply troubled and moved by Nora's situation.

"When? When? When can I leave?" asked Nora.

"I don't know. Soon — I think soon. I should just have to do some paperwork. But I don't know, I just don't know ..."

"Please, please, please don't forget me! Please, please don't leave me here!"

"I won't. Trust me!"

Then he left. He was in a state of mild shock as he left the school, just beginning to comprehend the extent of the injustice done to Nora. Nora herself had no choice but to trust him. Of course, she could not sleep that night or the following day: her excitement was too great. She tried to read, she tried to do some work around the wards, but it was all quite impossible. She could only think about life beyond the walls, of a life of freedom, of the life that she had not known for — how many years?

But by the end of the day she had become depressed. She realized that it might take days, weeks, months before she could go. She realized that it all depended on Farley, whom she hardly knew at all. He might have abandoned her already for all she knew, he might do nothing at all. And the following night she could not sleep either, but no longer because of excitement; she now felt something akin to damnation — eternal, boundless damnation: she had fallen directly from heaven into hell.

But Farley was there the next morning. He had the papers he needed. She would be out in an hour. But what to wear? She owned no clothes, not a thing of her own at all. In the end she had to borrow a dress from a fellow inmate before she could walk out the doors with Farley. The only other thing she took with her, concealed beneath her dress, was a smuggled, dog-eared copy of a book from the school's library, *lightly i dance the rivers of my life* by Elizabeth Morrow Wright.

(iii)

The world that Nora McPherson now entered was radically different from that which she left twelve years before. Before, her life was centered on her parents and on their spacious and comfortable home in Boston, where music, art, and learning were the stuff of everyday life. Elizabeth and Roger were her windows onto the outside world, and also the protectors from its cruel or thoughtless incursions upon Nora's well-being. Now she was alone: after a short stay with Farley she lived by herself in a small apartment in a suburb of Los Angeles. She was now a grown woman, and one who, had it not been for her 'sister', would have been considered quite attractive to others. However, she had completely missed the 'normal' social experiences of adolescence and young adulthood and was in many ways still a child. She was thus forced to cope, alone and without the experience of her peers, in a world which she had come, with good reason, to distrust. Her only compensation, if that is what it was, was her trust fund, which in spite of the inroads of Elias Whitmore's attorney, had grown to over half a million dollars and was still increasing from royalties and interest payments. At least she did not have to worry about her material existence.

Farley helped her somewhat, during the first few months. He took a lively and friendly interest in her and taught her basic things about living in a big city. As her savior, she trusted him inordinately, unlike anyone else. Sensitive and generous, he tried to live up to this trust, but eventually his own interests took him elsewhere, to another city, and he gradually drifted out of Nora's life.

During the first six months of her new life, Nora alternated between periods of intense physical activities out of doors — long walks, swimming, tennis with Farley, even horse-back riding, a new activity for her — and periods of

solitary intellectual activity in her apartment — mostly reading, but sometimes drawing, sometimes writing poetry. Her
excitement and wonder about the world were boundless,
and their expression often hauntingly childlike.   Though
Nora spent most of her time alone, there was certainly within her a formless yet deep longing for companionship. But
not only did she lack the experiences or models to give shape
to these feelings, but likewise the knowledge or experience to
seek their fulfillment. And behind everything was still the
fear — never uttered, hardly conscious that a stranger's
whim might suddenly and without justification, land her
once more in the 'concentration camp.'

It was Farley who suggested that she go to college. She
resisted the idea at first, recalling her schooldays as a child,
her education with Roger, recalling the Eastern State School.
She preferred to teach herself at home.

But Farley persisted, and trusting him, she allowed herself to be persuaded. And once she had made the decision,
undertaken that course, she pursued it wholeheartedly. Her
first stage of instruction was a nearby community college.
Here she found, for the first time, finally, what she had
longed for for so many years, what she had not experienced
since her parents' home. She immersed herself totally in
learning, immersed herself completely in its excitement. She
scarcely even noticed the often standoffish or unfriendly attitude of her fellow students towards her. She found finally
the direction, the encouragement that she had been lacking
on her own.

As a student, she was inexhaustible, she excelled. She
undertook a simultaneous study of literature, history, and
science. She was scarcely even aware of the examinations,
the grades, the distinctions she was achieving. She found the
tests they gave her too easy, so she made up her own. She
read and wrote far beyond the requirements of her curricu-

lum. She avoided boredom in the lecture hall by switching her attention back and forth between textbooks and lecturer, listening to the latter only when something new or interesting was being discussed. She pestered her professors with questions and for help on her special projects.

Later she transferred to a large state university, completed degrees in both history and biology in record time and went on to graduate study in neurobiology. Here, too, she worked with distinction, studying the chemical and electrical activity of the human brain during sleeping and dreaming, and was awarded a doctorate with honors. About the same time, unbeknownst to any of her colleagues, she privately published a volume of her poetry, with illustrations by herself, under the pseudonym of Nadine McPherson Wright. What were these poems? They were mostly celebrations of the exuberance and splendor of the natural world, of the cycles of nature, of freedom, of the enquiring mind that transcends physical limitations, that fearlessly questions and searches and uncovers. And filled with many vivid and powerful images, often with a dreamlike quality, of a mystical bent perhaps, whose significances are still puzzling. This work, and two other early volumes that Nora subsequently published, remained obscure for many decades; only now are they beginning to receive some of the recognition that they deserve.

Such was the more visible part of Nora's life during those years, her intellectual and academic pursuits. But what of her emotional, her psychic, her spiritual development? Anything that may be said about that can only be surmised, for there is no one who claims to have known Nora intimately during the years after she left the Eastern State School. It is very likely that Nora's social development had in many ways been stunted by her confinement in the 'concentration camp'. How could it have been otherwise? Thus we may imagine a young woman of twenty-two years and apart from the peculiarity of her 'sister', physically a beautiful woman, strongly resembling her mother, though with darker hair and fuller face — we may imagine a young woman, handsome, healthy, vigorous, brilliant of mind, totally self-possessed, who had never had a friend (other than her parents), never a peer, never known anyone who regarded her and whom she could regard as an equal. Most of her relationships at the Eastern State School had been of a helping nature, in which she provided support and assistance to someone far less fortunate than herself. It is questionable whether anyone had ever even tried to understand her, let alone succeeded. Probably the person who had come closest to that was Cynthia Wexler, her cellmate, who had died when Nora was seventeen. And so if Nora craved understanding or affirmation from her fellow humans, she had little cause to expect it to be forthcoming. Indeed, all of her experiences of the last twelve years and some of those before spoke to the contrary: She was different; she was a freak; the rest of the world, for reasons that were incomprehensible, seemed determined to confine her, to degrade her; the best she could hope for was not understanding or affection, but merely tolerance and benign neglect. For her, love had died with Elizabeth and Roger, and if other people seemed at times disposed to be friendly, it invariably proved to be only that: mere seeming.

Not that she was indifferent to those around her. On the contrary, her need for people was intense, yet at the same time she clearly saw that even her casual connections to others were far stronger than what anyone felt towards her. And so she came to expect to be called upon to give without receiving. This state of affairs certainly distressed her, even while she recognized its roots in her long isolation; but how much of it was due to that experience and how much was inborn — neither Nora nor anyone else would have been able to say.

Her poems sometimes spoke of a love — personal, intense, and unabashedly physical — towards another person, never named. Whether these were actual persons whom Nora encountered, or fictitious creations of her own psyche, we shall never know. No one ever inquired while Nora was living, and now the opportunity to do so is past. All we can say is that no one has ventured a reasonable guess as to who this person or persons might have been.

Upon completion of her highly acclaimed doctoral work on brain functioning during dreaming — she was still not yet thirty years old — Nora received several offers from universities around the country and abroad. She had her pick of choice positions in which she could pursue her research unhindered. She had finally, it appeared, overcome any remaining prejudice against her due to her physical appearance.

But Nora, to the surprise of her colleagues, chose to accept none of these offers. Instead, she quit the academic world entirely, abruptly and without explanation. Within a year she had become part of a new circus company, the Circus Mignese.

(iv)

It was either impossible or incredibly easy to see Alfonso Mignese in those days, assuming that he was available. He had an assistant by the name of Ignazio Testini, who happened to be a mute, and who always knew where Mignese was to be found. Without Testini's cooperation, no outsider could make their way to Mignese, who rarely used his office. How his assistant came to his decisions was unclear to anyone else except perhaps to Mignese, who trusted him implicitly. Testini would determine almost immediately, however, whether to turn a visitor away, to refer them to someone else in the company, or to lead them to Mignese. It seemed to be more a matter of the person's manner and state of mind rather than the stated nature of their business.

When Nora was directed to Ignazio Testini, she did not even state her reason for wanting to see the chief. She said simply: "I wish to speak with Alfonso Mignese." Perhaps it was her manner, her unshakeable, queenly self-confidence which convinced Testini to grant her wish immediately and without hesitation. Perhaps it was the concealed form of her 'sister', covered for the moment by a scarf, but a clear indication of something unusual. At any rate, Testini did nothing more than scan her face for an instant before turning and leading her to the master. "In there", his gestures said plainly, as he pointed to the door of a small mobile building. He did not even enter with her. As she stepped up to the door, Nora threw back the scarf, revealing her sister's placidly sleeping face. Then she knocked and entered.

Alfonso Mignese glanced up, then stood up as the door opened. He had been engaged in investigating a malfunctioning piece of machinery which lay partially disassembled on the floor beside him. Up until that moment, Nora had had no idea of what he looked like. The person that she saw appeared to be a short, slight adolescent of no more than seventeen years; with not very long, curly, black hair above a high, faintly-lined forehead; with well-defined yet delicate, almost feminine features; very fair, clear skin; not very broad, but full, deep red and sensuous lips. The faintest black fuzz on cheeks and chin prefigured a beard. The eyes were what captivated Nora: set deep within their sockets, they were a pure, light blue with just a hint of green: penetrating, open, gentle, curious.

Actually, at the time, Mignese was in his early thirties. He had reached his full growth of just five feet two inches at the age of sixteen, and, physically, scarcely changed thereafter. It is said, in fact, that he retained his boyish features and curly black hair until within one month of his death, at the age of nearly ninety, when his hair suddenly turned white and his face became lined. That is quite possibly true, for photos of him, taken over forty years apart show scarcely any change. Perhaps the hairline is a bit higher in the later shot, the eyes set a bit deeper, the face almost imperceptibly thinner, but otherwise the two pictures might well have been taken on two successive days, or under slightly different lighting conditions. It was also said of Alfonso Mignese that he was immensely strong, that he never or scarcely ever slept, that he spoke a dozen languages with ease, that he preferred to travel and wander about incognito, allowing himself to be taken for a child, etc. etc. He also died penniless, and reportedly, in a fit of laughter. The stories are many ...

As Nora entered the room, Alfonso Mignese rose up from the floor where he had been squatting, wiped his hands on his trousers as he stepped towards her, and was about to proffer her his hand when he looked down at it, decided that it was really too filthy after all, and shook instead an imaginary hand in the air as he smiled up at Nora — she was a good six inches taller than he — and said: "I am Alfonso

Mignese."

"Nora", she said, "Nora McPherson", and also shook an imaginary hand and returned his smile. Their eyes dwelt silently and warmly on each other for at least several seconds, before Mignese's moved to the side, rested placidly and curiously on the other head as he asked:

"Your sister sleeps always?" Never before had anyone chosen that term on their own — this man knew instantly.

"Always", said Nora, her pleasure growing.

"Does she dream?" asked Mignese.

"Yes" was all she answered.

"She tells you her dreams?"

"Yes."

"I understand."

* * * * * * * * * *

Exactly when it was decided that Nora was to be a part of the troupe is not clear. Very likely it was already implicit in their first words to each other, their first smiles of recognition. Maybe Ignazio Testini knew it when he saw Nora for the first time. What is certain is that Nora and Alfonso spent their first three days together in almost continual, though interrupted, conversation. Nora had intruded at a very busy time — actually hardly any time was scarcely less busy in those days — yet this did not hinder in the least their getting to know each other. Mignese simply dragged Nora about with him for three days straight, going about his work, meeting with performers and workmen, making preparations for the show, assembling and setting up equipment. As the hours passed, Nora began helping more and more; by the end of the first day she had already been accepted as having an important though still somewhat unclear role in the company. And as they moved about and worked, their interchange continued unabated, interrupted constantly to be sure, but never losing its thread for very long, sometimes flowing into long monologues by one or the other, sometimes distilled to a rapid, staccato exchange of single words or phrases, question/response or statement/counterstatement. Their words flowed with their work, and with the thoughts and feelings and experiences they shared. A thought might be cut off in mid-sentence by a sudden demand from outside, then continued five minutes or an hour later without loss of continuity or momentum, then be cut off again, then be taken up again. At night, while most of the company slept, their interchange would continue in the quiet of Mignese's quarters, by the light of a single candle, uninterrupted for long hours at a time. Sometimes Nora's body would demand that she rest, for half an hour, an hour at a time. But Mignese was never very far away, and no sooner would she open her eyes and rise but they would be right back where they left off. One time, Mignese sat down against a packing crate, closed his eyes for a moment, and was out for two hours. But Nora was right beside him when he woke up again.

Finally, after over three days, they were both totally exhausted. But the first night's performance had gone well and everything seemed to be running smoothly. So finally they withdrew, both of them together, to Mignese's quarters, and he gave word that they were not to be disturbed until further notice. Their last hour or more had been spent in a state of almost continual laughter.

They slept soundly in each other's arms for twelve hours, through that day and into the evening, and, except perhaps in their dreams, chastely. Their overwhelming need at that point was merely to restore the physical vitality of their bodies. That restored itself in due time, through the magic of sleep. Then they began the second day of their life together, this one, too, lasting three ordinary days, three of the days on the outside, which, for the moment, they did not feel any need to venture out into at all. And as their first day had

been spent in almost constant speech, their second was nearly speechless: What they now wished to convey could only
be said by hands and skin and lips, by eye speaking to eye,
by heartbeat and breath, by life's fire flowing through two
bodies as one, by two spirits trying to reach out and touch
directly. To try to recount any of this in words would be
hopeless.

They emerged finally. They had been missed; their energy, their understanding and judgment had been missed, but
their associates had carried on the work competently and
successfully in their absence. Apparently too, Ignazio Testini
had on his own accord given suggestions that others took to
be directives from Mignese.

Nora's coming marked a change in the nature of the
Circus Mignese, though one which was not to become evident for another several years. Until her time, the troupe had
consisted of a small but superb group of performers, whose
renown was not great by some standards, but who had been
noted and acclaimed by all who had seen them, and whose
success, at least in a modest way, seemed to be insured.
Nora's collaboration gave the company a vision and a purpose which it had not had before, although Mignese had perhaps unconsciously glimpsed it. She permitted him to give
utterance and wings to his own vision, enriched and aug-
mented it with her own, giving it a breadth and a power that
it had not previously known. He gave her a ready-made and
totally unique stage on which to exercise her own genius,
sensitivity, and remarkable practical energy. She brought
into the company a wealth of new talent, including many
having unique physical abilities that had once made them
outcasts like herself.

Their collaboration transformed that company. No
longer was it merely a performing group; it became something akin to a nomadic community, a tribe, a wandering

nation whose borders transcended the imaginary political, religious, or racial divisions that men have tried to inscribe on the earth's surface. It was a nation whose territory was not physical, but of the heart and spirit. And wherever it went, for over fifty years, it left behind it, not just colorful posters and fond memories, but an inkling, a vision, of a different kind of world, in which diversity was honored, differences nurtured, and the quality of a human being was not judged by the shape of their body, the hue of their skin, or the peculiarities of their traditions.

This is really, then, only the beginning of Nora's story; or rather, it is the end of her private and personal story and the beginning of her public one. From that time forward, her life and her story became commingled with and inseparable from Alfonso's and that of the circus that they created together. The stories of that circus are endless; some of its performers became universally known, others remain nameless and obscure. Thus the strands of Nora's life are forever intimately intertwined with those of thousands of others, many of them legendary in their own right. No volume of words could possibly do justice to who they were, their joys and anguish, their achievements and failures, their lives and their deaths. But surely, their spirit still hovers about the great halls and coliseums each time when the house lights dim, the audience hushes, and the impresario steps out into the brilliant circle of light ...

(Epilogue)

As we know, Nora's and Alfonso's work together continued for more than fifty years, until their deaths, within weeks of one another. Their company came into being at a time of great challenge and change, and it spanned two disparate eras. When they began, it was a desperate age of contentiousness and conflict and diminishing hopes. Nations were still armed to the teeth against one another. Ancient animosities flared constantly, threatening periodically to erupt into global warfare. The elites of the world and their armies struggled to maintain control of the dwindling resources needed for their opulent lifestyles. The dispossessed masses of humanity were growing restless, increasingly conscious of the disparity between the fruits of their own labor and that of their wealthy commensals. Race hatred and distrust, famine and war, were universally condemned, yet seemed endemic. Refugees seeking succor and relief from suffering were turned away or imprisoned. At the same time, the living body of the planet was increasingly ravished by the abuse and disregard of humans who treated it exclusively as a resource to be exploited. Mass extinctions were underway. The natural world that humankind depended on for its sustenance was withering and dying, the very air and waters of life becoming fouled, even as the world's population was hurtling out of control, towards a predictable yet seemingly inevitable catastrophe.

It was indeed a great historical crisis and very nearly a deadly one; but in the end, it proved to a healing crisis. And by the time the company Circus Mignese was dispersed — or more correctly, gave way to its many successors — it was a different era. Their company reflected and was part of, helped even to bring about, the great changes that took place. Nora's and Alfonso's grandchildren came of age in a world in which the great armies had been disbanded and the human-drawn borders of the past consigned to history, replaced by the natural divisions created by the earth's rivers and mountains and deserts. The cities, those once desperate collections of distressed humanity, began to be transformed and dismantled. The decimated forests were replanted. Much had been irretrievably lost, but the vitality of the whole still abides. The work of repair and regeneration goes on still.

Nora's legacy touched not just the three children that she bore, but the thousands who had been part of the circus, and the multitudes that their lives had touched. In the course of a career that lasted more than half a century, she managed to publish numerous volumes of her own writing, which stands as her own private, personal contribution. To this written legacy one must also add the hundreds of volumes, and the countless films and recordings of that circus and of its many luminaries. And then there are the many successors to their own circus that she helped midwife, and which still flourish.

In one of her last letters, to her great-grandson, a youth who had been left crippled by a cruel accident, she related some of her own personal trials and offered a perspective on her life. She wrote: "I and my sister had the luck to be born on this planet as one person, in one body. There were tears enough, but on the whole I have found that it is a fair place to be. If I could, I would do it again and again. All I can say to you is that if you have the luck to walk for a while beneath the sun, remember that every day is a miracle, and that every step is sacred."

Alfonso and Nora are buried near to each other, in a meadow not far from their home. There are no tombstones on their simple graves, but Nora had once written for herself an epitaph, never used. It said simply

Here Lie
Nora Wright McPherson
Nadine McPherson Wright
Sisters
Inseparable Companions

Colophon

Cerek is the author of several collections of short stories, and has also translated the works of other writers from German and Spanish. Besides writing fiction, he has worked as a mathematician, software engineer, janitor, woodworker, and bookbinder. He spent his early years on the Texas Gulf Coast. Refusing to serve in the war in Southeast Asia, he lived in exile in Europe for some years. After returning to the United States, he settled on the shores of the Salish Sea, the great inland sea of the Pacific Northwest where he lives today within sight of water and mountains.

Michael McCurdy, a master of the arts of scratchboard and wood engraving, has illustrated many books for adults and children. He lives and works in Western Massachusetts.

The stories in *Water Flowing Over Stone* were selected from some twenty years of work. This edition is set in Palatino and printed on Glatfelter Supple Opaque paper. In addition to the Trade Paperback edition, a Limited Deluxe edition of one hundred numbered copies is available, with hand-marbled end papers, bound and signed by the author.

Yggdrasil is the World Tree of ancient Northern European mythology. Its branches extend over every land, and it serves as a bridge between the worlds of mankind, gods, and other beings.

Inquiries concerning this book should be directed to Yggdrasil Books, Box 399, Waldron, Washington 98297, USA.